'Do you come from an acting family? I should think you do. I sincerely believed your portrayal of innocence.'

Antonia shuddered. She knew what was coming.

'You lied to me when I asked if we'd met before. You were that incompetent girl who argued and fussed when I needed to be here operating.'

She hung her head, and found herself unable to speak.

Rolf was raging on. 'Now I find you're a woman who has misinterpreted the essential qualities of a nurse. A good nurse should be warm and compassionate, not hot and passionate!'

'How dare you?' she shot back. 'If you'd been a woman alone, and a stranger suddenly shot into your car, you'd be afraid. And you didn't exactly come across as reasoned and coherent.'

Her eyes met and held his. Their eyes remained locked for some seconds. The short time seemed to go on for an eternity. He was burning into her soul, and she was afraid.

Sara Burton was convent educated and trained as a physiotherapist at a school in the Midlands. She has worked in England, Scandinavia and North America and received her B.Sc. in Physical Therapy from a Western Canadian University. Currently she is engaged in independent research related to partial dislocation of joints in the lower limbs. She is a bird fancier with a special interest in homing pigeons.

Previous Titles

DR ROSKILDE'S RETURN
A MEDICAL OPINION

EXPERT TREATMENT

BY

SARA BURTON

MILLS & BOON LIMITED
ETON HOUSE   18–24 PARADISE ROAD
RICHMOND   SURREY   TW9 1SR

*First published in Great Britain 1990
by Mills & Boon Limited*

© Sara Burton 1990

*Australian copyright 1990
Philippine copyright 1990
This edition 1990*

ISBN 0 263 77078 8

*Set in 11½ on 13 pt Linotron Baskerville
03-9012-39132
Typeset in Great Britain by Centracet, Cambridge
Made and printed in Great Britain*

CHAPTER ONE

'DRIVE to the Royal Hospital. It's urgent!'

Antonia had been waiting for the red traffic-light to turn to green, when the door of her compact car had been rudely wrenched open and immediately banged shut again. Now a tall strange man sat by her side in the front passenger seat.

He was covered in plaster dust and other builder's debris, and his wild eyes stared out from his face like those of a bird of prey. His breathing was laboured and ragged.

Her nurse's training came to the front of her mind, dispelling all traces of fear in this unusual situation. 'Have you hurt yourself?' she asked.

She thought he was holding his right shoulder very stiffly. Her fingers attempted to gently palpate the part.

Immediately he jerked round and looked her full in the face. 'I'm not the patient. I'm the surgeon,' he snapped.

His reply was so unreal and unexpected that she almost laughed in disbelief. Her blue eyes widened as she took in his whole appearance.

Dressed in reinforced dirty steel-capped boots, torn faded blue jeans, and a well-worn old black T-shirt, he looked like a navvy straight from a building site.

'Don't just sit there,' he ground out. 'Get this thing moving. The Royal, I said.'

'Is it April the first?' she spoke as if half to herself. 'If you're a real surgeon why can't you drive yourself to the hospital? And if your car's out of action for some reason, then the police will always give you a flying squad escort.'

'You stupid girl! I can't drive myself because I've got a bird in my bonnet——'

Now Antonia really did laugh. 'Don't you mean a bee in your bonnet, or better still a bat in your belfry?'

'I meant exactly what I said,' came the aggressive reply. 'And at this ungodly hour of six o'clock on a Sunday morning, you're my best bet. You're readily available.'

Antonia didn't like his choice of words or the vicious twist of his mouth as he made his delivery. She began to feel afraid and to curse herself for not having locked her car door.

Strange people did roam the streets, and she was new to this town. And, although the district here looked select, any house might have been converted to a halfway home for psychiatric patients.

Trying desperately to play for time and gain some control of the situation, she asked a question which sounded silly to herself as soon as she had said it. 'Do you live in that big white house?'

It was a huge building close to the main road, and she could see by the numerous bells on the front door that it was a conversion into flats.

'I own Hawksworth,' came the exasperated reply. 'But I've no time for idle social talk. You have a choice. Either you put this car into gear right now and we drive, or I'll push you out on to the pavement and I'll commandeer this thing!'

She believed every word he said, but sat rigidly in her seat.

He took her hand in a manacle-tight grip and thrust it towards the ignition key. The car had stalled on his entry. But his fingers were immaculate, with short well-clipped nails, and they were as clean as if he had scrubbed them for hours. This man did not add up. His whole presence, so near and forbidding, made her shudder.

The look in his grey eyes was as intense as white light. Antonia looked away and lost no time in obeying.

She turned the key, the engine revved and they were on their way, speeding along a wide tree-lined road. Although she drove, she knew she was under his control.

For a moment she could not speak. Her throat was constricted. It was as well that she knew the way to the Royal. And she had only found that out minutes previously.

Antonia Moore was to start work as a staff nurse on the orthopaedic ward at eight the following morning. Being a conscientious girl, she had just sorted out the quickest way to work from her small flat, and before this encounter she had been on her way home for breakfast.

The stranger by her side was alert, and surveying the road ahead with eagle eyes. 'Left here,' he ordered.

'But the way is straight on——'

'Left!' His hand grabbed the steering-wheel and pulled hard down. They took the bend at a hairpin angle.

Fury got the better part of Antonia. 'Are you practising for Le Mans? You're mad!'

'Right! Right here!' The steering-wheel came under his dominant control again. She was petrified. 'Take the right fork now.'

'But——'

'Stop this incessant babble,' he ordered. 'Right now my colleague is performing a traumatic amputation. Some poor bastard is trapped in the cab of his lorry. I need to be in theatre, and quickly. I'll have to reconstruct, so that the prosthetist can make a reasonable limb. . . *You* are wasting precious seconds!'

The mental image of mutiliation coupled with the authoritative force of his command made her gulp. Could this man really be a surgeon? Cars, trees and houses flashed by in a blur.

'The traffic-lights are red ahead,' she croaked.

'Straight ahead.'

It was the reply that she had expected, and, hooting loudly, straight through they sped. Now the hospital was in sight. Antonia's reflexes were razor-sharp as she took the entrance at speed and applied squealing brakes at the rear of an emergency ambulance.

Before her car had come to a halt the stranger leapt out, turned slightly to slam her car door and ordered, 'Now get out of here!'

If Antonia had thought she was transporting a top surgeon, the words on his T-shirt brought that idea crashing to earth: BARE BARBER-SURGEON. She took it in instantly.

What real surgeon in their right mind ran about with that emblazoned on their chest? No one she had ever known.

She watched incredulously as he sped like a bullet to the main doors. All the pent-up power that had been by her side was now in motion.

The wail of another approaching ambulance made her put the car in gear and reverse out of the way. She cleared the entrance just in time, and when she was safely in a parking space she leant on the steering-wheel and shuddered as she watched a patient with a drip being rushed in.

Her whole frame trembled as she witnessed the flurry of activity, and then just as suddenly they were out of sight and she was alone in the car park.

She tried to steady herself by taking deep breaths from her diaphragm. Slowly she regained her equilibrium. As she pushed her full fringe of nut-brown hair off her forehead she sat back and exhaled audibly.

The encounter had been one of the most frightening in her life. No, not quite, she thought, and mentally blotted out the past.

All the same, it had been a swift and traumatic incident. That commanding man had literally hijacked her. And she hadn't even received a 'thank-you' for her part.

Who was that stranger? Her mind turned on the subject. She had no idea, except that he probably worked here at the Royal. He knew something about surgery. But no surgeon would allow a mere bird to stop him using his car in an emergency.

The only seemingly solid piece of information he had given her about himself was that he owned Hawksworth. Antonia determined to do a bit of detective work. If she found the house, she could ask if the owner really was a surgeon and if he had been called out on an emergency.

Soon she was back at the crossroads where the extraordinary incident had taken place. Slowly she drove up towards a turreted church with spires, and there on the left she saw Hawksworth.

It was no ordinary house, more like a mansion from the Gothic era. Its name was boldly carved into the stone of one of the pillars at the entrance.

Antonia parked her car and walked through the entrance. The house itself had been partly obscured by a high copper beech hedge. But as she followed the sweeping drive she saw a building of stone, built with solidity and strength.

The façade had three pointed triangular sections. This gave the impression of a great towering height, topped with fantastic spires. The windows were large and subdivided into smaller elements, giving a delicate and refined impression.

But it was the stone carvings that really took her breath away. Three giant hawks' heads adorned the front and there were even stone gargoyles at the sides. The whole gave the impression of power and richness. The master of Hawksworth must certainly be a man of distinction, Antonia conceded.

'Huh. . .' she said aloud, and thought of her barber surgeon again. He'd left plaster dust all over her car seat and the floor. If he really was the owner of this mansion, then some trace of his dirty footprints would be visible.

She scanned the drive. It was black and newly tarmacked—no tell-tale evidence there. At the front door she surveyed the steps. Everywhere was immaculate and clean.

Feeling bold, she looked for the front door bell. But there was none. So she lifted the brass knocker and knocked twice.

At this point she began to feel a little foolish. As she tried to put the incident into words in her mind it sounded crazy and completely incomprehensible. She waited and waited, but no one answered her knocking.

No cars were on the drive. Perhaps the real owner was away. She peeped through the hedge into the grounds at the rear of the house—there was no garage there. She was thwarted. But she believed for sure now that her hijacker was not the owner here.

He was probably some theatre technician, she told herself, as she left the grounds. And someone with an exaggerated self-opinion. No doubt he had fantasies of being a surgeon. His dreams were probably filled with images of himself playing the part of Mr Excitement.

Nothing about him was like a real doctor. He was nothing like Lindain—her darling Lindain who had been such a support and help to her following the sudden death of her parents in that boating accident.

And Antonia had loved Lindain so much that she had given up the opportunity of being sister on her old orthopaedic ward in the hospital where she had trained. She had followed him here to this Cotswold town.

Yes, Dr Lindain Smythe would put that barber surgeon in his place. She'd tell Lindain all about the incident tonight when he returned from his course in London.

She had hated being parted from Lindain, even if it was only for a few months before her job at the Royal had been secured. But, come December, and on her birthday, he had promised that they would become officially engaged. And when they were married they would sleep with their bodies entwined, and then she felt she would never be afraid of anything, not even the darkest night.

Back in her small flat on top of a butcher's shop and opposite a respectable-looking pub, Antonia flicked a duster over the furniture and felt pleased.

She checked her watch several times and hoped that Lindain wouldn't arrive too late. As the last light faded from the summer sky she became afraid and worried in case he had been in a car crash. Then her mind focused back on her early morning hospital ride and she wondered if the patient she had seen in the ambulance was recovering.

Every light in her flat blazed. She knew it was an extravagance, but there was another reason why she wanted light. She had a fear of the dark.

In her childhood she could never sleep without her bedside lamp. She felt she would have outgrown this but for the incident down the coalmine. When she was a student a group of nurses had been escorted around a working mine. The idea was to show them what conditions the men worked in, and how important proper nursing and rehabilitation were to any injured miner.

But disaster had struck, some explosives had been incorrectly used and a young man had died, crushed to death before her eyes.

And ever since that time her fear of the dark was coupled with terror and death. Now it had become a fixated fear and developed into a full-blown phobia. But Antonia kept these things to herself, oddly ashamed that she was a nurse, but still could not cope.

A ring on her doorbell brought her back to present time, and she rushed down the narrow wooden stairs to open the door.

'Lindain—at last! I thought something had happened to you. You're so late.' She kissed him first and hugged him close.

'Ha. . . You have missed me, haven't you?' His expression was smug, but lost on Antonia as he brushed the hair from her cheek and kissed her.

Somehow Lindain's kisses were too short for Antonia's liking, and she was almost angry when he turned away and said, 'My car will be safe in this back alley, won't it? Why did you have to pick such an unsavoury spot to live?'

'It's not unsavoury,' she defended. 'And the neighbours have all been very welcoming to me.'

He didn't look completely convinced as he glanced back at his red sports car. She slipped her arm through his and they went upstairs. She wanted to know all about his course.

'Excellent.' His voice held a tone of importance. 'Those London consultants are first-rate. Much better than some of the old bodgers here in the country.'

She smiled to herself; she knew Lindain's aspirations were high. 'You'll be a London man one day, I'm sure.' She wanted to help him in every way. His help after her parents' funeral had been a lifeline.

As Lindain sipped his coffee and sat elegantly on her chesterfield he said, 'I'm whacked—that drive tonight was frightful. Of course, I came straight to see you, darling.'

After some more talk about his course on the difficulties of intubation he asked, 'And how was your day?'

Here was Antonia's opportunity to tell him about her barber surgeon. 'I was hijacked,' she said simply.

Lindain raised his eyes over the brim of his coffee-cup.

'Yes, really. Some builder-type man covered in plaster dust descended on me when I was out driving and ordered me to the Royal.'

'And I suppose, being the good little ministering angel that you are, you took him to Casualty and they put a plaster on his finger or something.'

Antonia felt put out. 'Nothing so normal. The man was something short of a maniac! He said he couldn't drive his car because there was a bird in it. He was extremely rude, we literally fought for the steering-wheel at one point. He was some jumped-up theatre technician or something. I knew he wasn't a real surgeon because of the slogan on his T-shirt—"Bare Barber-Surgeon".'

Lindain turned an unhealthy shade of parchment and started to choke on his coffee.

'Yes,' she continued, 'I knew you'd be angry.

Apart from being appallingly rude and overbearing, he tried to tell me that he was a surgeon about to perform a reconstruction on an amputee.'

Rage turned Lindain's handsome features ugly. He put down his coffee, then turned on Antonia, clasping her shoulders in a painful grip.

'You little fool! That was no workman. That was Mr Rolf McMaster, consultant orthopaedic surgeon!'

She stared at Lindain in disbelief. 'But——'

'But nothing. . .!' His voice rose to an unnatural pitch. 'McMaster's been in a foul mood all day. And your dawdling didn't help one jot!'

'I don't understand——'

Lindain jumped to his feet and began to pace the room, leaving Antonia alone and looking utterly dumbfounded. He rounded on her. 'You're damn right you don't understand!'

'But who in their right mind wears a T-shirt saying "Bare Barber-Surgeon"? That would be like a professor of physics running around the university with "Einstein Was a Woman" on his chest.'

'This is no time to be funny!' he almost yelled. 'Paré barber-surgeon—Paré. Can't you read, Antonia?'

'Not when the man was covered in dirt and

sweat. And anyway, who is Paré? I've never heard of him.'

Lindain stood square and thrust his hand through his floppy fair hair. 'Paré is McMaster's hero. He's always wittering on about him. To McMaster, Paré is as important as Pasteur, or Lister, or Hippocrates. Oh, he was some French teenager who came to Paris in the sixteenth century. He worked his way up from a barber's apprentice and eventually became surgeon to the King of France.'

Antonia felt a rising need to defend herself. 'But McMaster sounded like a lunatic to me, when he said he had a bird in his bonnet——'

'McMaster was officially on holiday renovating that mansion of his. He'd been away to see a stonemason, and during that time a blackbird had built her nest on the battery of his car.' Lindain covered his brow with one hand. 'Apparently McMaster had been working on his car and the bonnet was up and parts were scattered about the garage floor. The hospital called him in because he's so brilliant with amps.'

Antonia let out a low groan. So all the craziness was really rooted in reality! The only problem had been that she didn't know all these circumstances.

She spoke very quietly now. 'I thought surgeons always took particular care of their hands and never risked any sort of manual work.' Her voice trailed away.

'McMaster's hands are always pristine,' Lindain snapped. 'He wears surgical gloves and others when he's renovating.'

Sinking back on the chesterfield, Antonia saw the whole scene again. And yes, it was true, the surgeon's hands had been immaculate. She rubbed her wrist, as if feeling his manacle grip again. But something made her frown.

'How do you know all this, Lindain? You said that you'd come straight from the course to me.'

Instantly his expression became a blank. He hesitated momentarily. 'I did pop into the Royal, just for a short time. I was worried about a patient of mine. . . The grapevine was positively buzzing!'

Antonia's face began to crumple and tears began to well up into her eyes.

Lindain sat down by her side and put his arm around her shoulders. His assumed charm came to the front. 'Dry your eyes now. Look, we've got to work out some plan. A plan that will get me out of this mess that you've landed me in.'

She looked up into his eyes. 'I'll apologise, of course.'

'No.' Lindain's voice was firm. 'No, don't do

that—it might not be necessary. McMaster believes that the girl who gave him a lift was a teenager. You look so much older in uniform, and with your hair up. . .there's a good chance we'll get away with it. Let's just hope he never connects you with the drive.'

Taking Lindain's pocket handkerchief and wiping her nose, Antonia agreed.

'What about the patient?' she asked.

'The patient?'

'Yes, the one McMaster operated on. Did you hear how he was?'

To Antonia, Lindain's tone held a note of nastiness. 'McMaster had to revise the level of amputation by the time he was finally prepared to operate. The man has an above-knee amputation now. . .not a through-knee.'

Now Antonia felt waves of nausea well up inside her. She covered her mouth. Although she didn't know a great deal about amputations she knew enough. The higher the level, the more complicated the recovery, and the more difficulty in prosthetic fitting.

Rolf McMaster's words came back to her like a slap in the face. 'You are wasting precious seconds.' Had the time she had spent arguing with him made the difference?'

'Buck up, Antonia.' Lindain's words filtered through the fog of her mind. 'You can do it—

you can pull me through. You know, consultants' jobs aren't easy to find. And I'll need every senior consultant I know to give me backing when I've passed my exams.'

She was blind to all his faults, his peacock pride and his selfishness. And it was as if she didn't hear him. All she could think of was how she would face the patient in the morning, because her ward was the only orthopaedic one at the Royal. And, even more difficult, how would she face consultant surgeon Mr Rolf McMaster?

CHAPTER TWO

'GOODNESS, you're here early, Staff Nurse Moore! Personnel didn't keep you all morning filling in forms?'

Sister Cook stood up from her desk and they shook hands. As the introductions were being made Antonia decided she would like working with this sister. She was in her middle fifties, and, although her face was lined, it showed all her evident good nature.

Ward eight was very old-fashioned. It was the size of a football pitch and the huge windows towered upwards to the ceiling. Sister's desk was situated slap in the middle with beds all around, and even some in the centre aisle.

As Antonia had entered the ward she had wondered which patient was her amputee.

Sister said, 'You've missed report, so I'll give you a detailed briefing on each patient myself.' She laughed. 'It's unusual today—we're fully staffed, so I can afford to take my time with you.'

A smile flickered across Antonia's face. This hospital was no different from any other she had worked in.

Every time Sister pointed out a new patient on the ward and gave a history, Antonia's heart lurched. But not one was her amputee.

As Sister consulted the Kardex once more Antonia enquired, 'I heard that an emergency patient was brought in here yesterday. Is he on another ward?'

'Our Eddy, you mean.' Sister flicked over another section of Kardex. 'Ah, yes. He's in the sun-room.' She nodded her chin in the direction of the end of the ward, and Antonia recognised an extension that she hadn't noticed before.

Sister sighed. 'I've put him there to let him have a bit of peace and privacy. There are only two patients in that section.'

'Was he very badly injured?' Antonia tried to subdue her tone.

Sister Cook looked her square in the face. 'No experience is more shocking to anyone than loss of a limb.' She paused. 'There's something dreadfully final about it. . . It's the loss of a treasured part of the body. People don't appreciate a limb properly, until one's gone.'

Antonia knew all this and sat rigid and silent.

Looking up at the ceiling, and stroking her neck, Sister continued, 'Life isn't fair. Of course, being a nurse you know all about that. But this is a tragic case. Eddy was doing a friend a favour by transporting a lorry, and a child ran out into the road. Our Eddy swerved, missed the child but hit a tree. The child suffered nothing but shock, but Eddy got the raw end of the deal.'

Antonia held her breath.

'But our Eddy's a lucky boy—if you can believe that Lady Luck can appear at times like these.'

Eager to hear any good fortune in the circumstances, Antonia leaned forward.

'Yes. The hospital was able to call in the best orthopaedic surgeon I've ever known.' Sister nodded proudly. 'Rolf McMaster is a wonderful man and a brilliant surgeon. He has a special interest in amputees.' Sister sighed again. 'You know, Staff, I've seen many surgeons in my time, and frequently they hate to amputate. Sometimes they suffer emotional guilt after they've performed the operation, and then they avoid seeing the patient after surgery.'

'Mr McMaster isn't like that, then?' Antonia felt very relieved to hear that her commandeering surgeon was so different from the opinion she had first conceived.

'Dear me, no! He was here well into the night and again early this morning, checking on Eddy.'

Antonia ventured, 'And how is Eddy taking things?'

'Hard to say at this early stage. McMaster doesn't believe in patients suffering undue pain, particularly after such a trauma, so Eddy is fairly heavily under medication.' Sister peered closely into Antonia's eyes. 'Have you a special interest in nursing amputees? You seem particularly interested.'

'I haven't had a great deal to do with amps,' Antonia conceded. 'But I'm very keen to learn.' She gabbled on, 'My boyfriend is a doctor here, and he told me all about the case last night.'

Sister smiled knowingly. 'Ah, that's why we've been lucky enough to tempt you to work here at the Royal.'

'Yes.' Antonia lowered her eyelashes. 'We're unofficially engaged.'

'And which junior doctor will you marry?'

'Dr Lindain Smythe. He's an anaesthetist.' Antonia smiled warmly.

But Sister's face fell. 'Dr Lindain Smythe?'

'Yes—he's only been here a few months.'

Antonia couldn't understand why Sister looked so puzzled.

The telephone rang, interrupting their conversation. She sat back in her chair and looked towards the sun-room.

She heard Sister laugh. 'So you've heard I'm fully staffed, and you thought you'd poach someone off me!' Then, 'Well, I'll expect a mighty big favour off you some time. Yes. . .' Antonia saw

Sister look directly at herself. 'Yes, I've a new staff nurse here, I think she'll be very suitable.'

As Sister replaced the receiver she had a strangely conspiratorial smile. 'Outpatient Orthopaedic Clinic have a bit of a problem this morning—the sister in charge has had to go off sick. Would you mind lending a hand down there?'

'Not at all.' Antonia was eager to please. There would be enough time to see Eddy later, and, if the truth was known, she was very apprehensive about meeting him.

'You know how these clinics are run, I'm sure,' said Sister.

'Yes, I've assisted at quite a few.'

'And Mr McMaster's no problem. He's very affable and accommodating, especially with new staff.'

A hard knot began to grow in Antonia's throat. She hadn't expected such an early encounter with the surgeon. She sat transfixed.

Sister issued directions, but as Antonia still remained sitting her voice became stern. 'Run along now, Staff. No one ever keeps Mr McMaster waiting. You'll understand why the moment you set eyes on him.'

Outside the clinic entrance, Antonia felt her heart begin to flutter. Whatever she might feel when she saw McMaster, she had better make a concentrated effort to get on with him. And there was Lindain's future to think of.

The waiting-room was filled to capacity. She could see the reception office straight ahead. It looked empty.

The mental image of Rolf McMaster as she had first seen him flashed vividly into her mind. He wouldn't look anything like that this morning, she told herself.

Mentally she braced herself, but as she entered the office she halted in her tracks.

And there he was, sitting nonchalantly on a working surface that acted like a desk. She took his whole altered appearance in with one sweeping glance.

His hair was sooty black in colour, short and brushed straight back from his forehead. And his long eyelashes stood out against the dark smudges under his eyes. His eyebrows were black, straight and formidable even as he concentrated on sellotaping a torn, very worn patient file.

Here sat no navvy. His leather shoes were polished and shone like black glass. He wore a navy pin-striped suit, a sparkling white shirt and a black silk tie. All this, and his pristine starched white coat, proclaimed him to be the consultant that he undoubtedly was.

He spoke without looking up, as his long

elegant fingers worked on the file. 'There, as good a strapping job as you'd find on the ankle of any First Division footballer.'

That voice was very different from the one she had been subjected to in the car. It held warmth and fun and undeniable pride. No false modesty here, thought Antonia.

When he looked up she was confronted with brilliant grey eyes. They sparkled alive as he put down the folder, slid off the desk and came forward to welcome her with his hand outstretched.

'You're not Betty, our clerical assistant,' he said smoothly. As he walked towards her she was aware of his towering height and the breadth of his shoulders. She shook hands as if in a trance.

His finger touched her name-tag above her left breast. 'Staff Nurse A. Moore—welcome. I'm Mr McMaster. It was good of you to help out at such short notice.'

'Good morning, sir,' she said rather too formally. But she was only too glad that he hadn't recognised her.

Then those grey eyes narrowed, and his expression became curious. 'Haven't I seen you somewhere else before, Staff?'

She gulped. 'No, sir.'

'Hmm. . . But you still look very familiar.'

Being too eager to put him off this line of

questioning, she replied rather primly, 'I assure you, I'm not at all familiar.'

A chuckle caught in his throat and his eyes became mischievous. Standing with his legs wide apart and his hands thrust into his trouser pockets, pulling the material tight across his hips, he answered, 'Not at all familiar, eh?'

Antonia felt as if the ensuing silent seconds were like hours. She decided she didn't like him—certainly not in that positive masculine posture. He was the sort of man who played games, and she didn't intend to play.

Then his expression changed, and his smile was disarmingly handsome. 'You look like a good little Florence Nightingale to me. And that's the way I like my nurses. Patient care is a priority here. I've never tolerated nurses who are only working in a hospital to seek out and catch a good husband.'

She was stunned. She hadn't expected this line of talk. But so far she was safe; he hadn't recognised her.

He showed her the rooms in the clinic himself, carefully pointing out the different areas and explaining slowly and carefully the way he liked his clinic run.

And throughout the rest of the morning his behaviour was impeccable. If she looked at all flustered because she couldn't find things, he calmly found them for her. His voice was always unhurried and reassuring. She had to concede that he was very reasonable to work with.

When Antonia ushered in the last patient of the morning she knew there was going to be trouble.

Nigel Cluny was accompanied by his mother. And her whole manner proclaimed battle stations.

As Antonia showed Nigel where to sit on the plinth in the examination cubicle, Mrs Cluny began her attack.

'We're new to this area and district, Nurse. I've had a very difficult time getting an appointment for our Nigel. His GP said it wasn't necessary so soon after leaving his old consultant, but I insisted.' She nodded her head for emphasis.

Mrs Cluny was a big woman in her mid-forties. She was dressed in her finest regalia, and almost every piece of jewellery she possessed. In her hand she carried a large object carefully wrapped in black plastic.

'Nigel's got to be given a proper leg,' she began fiercely. She unwrapped the black plastic to reveal an artificial one. 'This one's no good, or at least he says it isn't.' She gave Nigel a withering look.

The young lad was thin and tall for his age. Antonia guessed that he was about sixteen. He sat on the plinth with his axillary crutches resting on his own leg, his expression one of mortified embarrassment.

'Slip off your trousers and your shoe and sock,' Antonia told him gently. She was about to raise the back of the plinth when Mrs Cluny started up again.

'This Mr McMaster. . . Is he any good, Nurse?' She raced on, 'I don't think our Nigel got a good deal where we lived before. You see, the hospital where they operated didn't have a prosthetics workshop. I believe that was the trouble. We only saw the limb-maker a couple of times, because we had to travel so far.'

Antonia sprang to Rolf McMaster's defence. 'Oh, this surgeon is very clever, Mrs Cluny. He has a special interest in patients with Nigel's condition. And the limb-fitting centre for the Midlands is attached to this hospital.'

Nigel stared blankly at his crutches, and Mrs Cluny said, 'It's about time we had a bit of luck.'

Making her escape quickly through the connecting door, Antonia saw Rolf McMaster reading through the heavy weight of notes that belonged to Nigel.

'Hmm. . .' He continued to read. 'This is a sad case. Two years ago, when young Nigel was fourteen, he came off the worse with an encounter with a piece of farm machinery.' He looked up. 'That's the trouble with increasing mechanisation in agriculture and industry. This could be difficult. Amputation at any age is hard to deal with, but at puberty as well. . .' He sighed.

Coming closer to the desk and keeping her voice low, Antonia explained about Mrs Cluny's attitude.

Rolf McMaster tapped the patient file with the tip of his gold pen. 'Ah. . .you are a good little scout, Staff Nurse A. Moore. That sort of information gives me a slight edge, and a few moments to prepare for the confrontation.' He smiled charmingly and asked, 'What's your first name? Ann? Andrea?'

'Antonia, sir.'

'Well, Antonia,' he stood up, 'let's see if I can satisfy both mother and son.'

On entering the cubicle he gave a no-nonsense, 'Good morning,' the sweep of his glance taking in Nigel first, and then Mrs Cluny. 'Mrs Cluny, I'm so glad you've come with your son.' He shook her hand warmly. 'It's such a pleasure seeing a member of the family being supportive.'

This worked instantly. Mrs Cluny beamed. A string of 'thank you, Doctor', followed, and she was only too willing to sit down in the chair that Rolf McMaster himself brought out for her.

He turned to Nigel, shok his hand and began, 'Lie back and let me examine your leg.'

Antonia let down the back-rest and rearranged the pillows. It was obvious even to her, and she had no real depth of knowledge about amputees, that Nigel's stump was far too short to be of any use in an artificial limb. Also there was deep and excessive scarring which would rub against the limb socket and cause pain and skin breakdown.

Rolf McMaster's hands were gentle yet skilful. 'Now, turn on your side, Nigel.' The boy obeyed, pushing the tails of his shirt between his legs, no doubt for modesty in his mother's presence. But this was hardly necessary as Rolf McMaster positioned his body as a screen, thus effectively lessening the lad's embarrassment.

But Mrs Cluny couldn't contain herself. 'What do you think, Mr McMaster? Can you fix Nigel up with a proper leg? It's a job he'll be needing soon. And no employer looks at anyone when they're. . .well. . .different.'

Rolf McMaster's expression didn't change as he turned and walked to the mother.

'I need to do a very thorough examination of Nigel,' he told her quietly. 'Very thorough, you understand. It needs to be quite intimate if I'm to do the best for him. So would you mind sitting in the waiting area? Nurse will take you, and come and collect you when I need to explain everything to you.'

She stood up smartly. 'Of course, sir, I'll do

exactly what you say. I can see Nigel's going to get proper treatment now we've found you.'

Antonia had no trouble taking Mrs Cluny away. 'He's going to be all right with this doctor, I can tell,' the mother affirmed sagely.

Quickening her step, Antonia returned to the examination cubicle, and heard Rolf McMaster say, 'And would you like a new leg, Nigel?'

The lad was silent for a moment. 'I'm all right as I am. I don't see how they can make one to fit.' His brow was crinkled and serious. 'It's such an effort to move the thing, and I sweat in it, then it rubs the skin and makes it sore. No, I don't want another.'

Rolf McMaster rubbed his upper lip. 'You're quite right, Nigel.' He took a deep audible breath. 'Do you find you can get about easily on your crutches?'

'Yeah, fine.' The lad looked relieved that the question of another artificial limb was now out of the way. 'I ride my pushbike as well as anyone. I even fixed up some clips, and my crutches fit perfectly into them.'

Rolf McMaster nodded in approval.

'Oh, yeah,' Nigel looked sullen, 'my mum says I've got to ask for a new pair of crutches. I broke these, but I fixed them up myself.'

Antonia fetched the pair of wooden crutches

from the corner and handed them to Rolf McMaster.

'But these are beautifully decorated!' He produced a small magnifying glass from his breast pocket and held it near to some ornate metal bands surrounding the split in one part of the wood. 'See this, Staff?' He held out one for Antonia. 'Now don't you think this metalwork is breathtaking? The workmanship is as good as a jeweller's precision.'

Looking closely, Antonia saw that the metal bands weren't plain hoops, but elegantly formed snakes biting their own tails. 'Yes, it's exquisite.'

'Did you do this too, Nigel?' Rolf McMaster wanted to know.

'Yeah. Dad's a welder and he taught me. He brings home scraps from the factory.' He looked at his work proudly.

'And what's this earring?' Rolf McMaster's elegant finger touched a silver cross hanging from Nigel's left ear.

Nigel hooked it out and handed it over. 'It's a crucifix,' he explained. 'I've made it in the shape of two nails.'

'Brilliant!' The surgeon spoke admiringly, turning the item over in his hand. Then in a serious tone, 'Have you thought what you'll do when you leave school?'

'I want to be a welder like Dad.'

'Wouldn't you rather make jewellery?'

Nigel's face creased into a sly grin. 'Yeah, and have beautiful women wear it.' He looked down on the floor. 'But, as Mum says, you can't make a living from art.'

The consultant said nothing for a moment, then he handed back the crucifix. 'Get dressed, Nigel.' Turning to Antonia, he said, 'Bring Mrs Cluny in again. I'll come back and have a talk with her in a minute.'

'What's been going on?' the mother wanted to know as soon as she saw Antonia. She seemed impatient when Antonia tactfully told her that the consultant would explain everything.

As they passed the clerical office she heard Rolf McMaster laugh into the phone. 'No, Hans, I don't want another necklace for a lady. But I think I've got a jewel for you.'

This made Antonia curious. What was he up to?

Mr McMaster confronted Mrs Cluny and Nigel with a ghost of a twinkle in his eyes. He held a picture of a skeleton in his hands. 'I'm sorry to tell you, Mrs Cluny, that an artificial limb would be impossible to fit on Nigel.'

All the woman's fight seemed to go out of her as she sighed, 'Oh, dear!' She even looked physically smaller.

Rolf McMaster took time and pains to explain

to her. 'And you see,' he pointed to the pelvis of the skeleton in the picture, 'Nigel doesn't have the basic eight centimetres of length left in his leg in order to use a prosthesis.'

'Well, I do see now.' The mother looked grief-stricken.

'Leave the old leg with us,' Rolf McMaster said gently. 'The spare parts can be used again for someone else. So it won't have been an entire waste.'

'I'll keep his shoe,' she said quietly. 'Although I don't know why. Perhaps it would be useful to someone—they cost so much. And he doesn't wear it, it's brand-new.'

Antonia unpacked the limb and wrapped the shoe in the plastic bag. 'What about the National Odd Shoe Association, sir?' she ventured.

'What's that?' The surgeon looked interested.

'It's for people with odd-sized feet. They have a file, and Nigel might be paired up with someone who has no use for a shoe for his size foot.'

He seemed delighted. 'Good idea. I'll look into that and let you know, Mrs Cluny.'

'Oh, good.' The mother tried to look pleased.

Now Rolf McMaster's voice changed. It held a note of triumph. 'But I do have a prescription for you, Nigel.'

The lad looked surprised.

'Present yourself at Hans Stein's in the High

Street on Saturday morning at nine o'clock. You have a job interview for a goldsmith's apprenticeship.' He handed the stunned lad a piece of paper with the details.

Turning to Mrs Cluny, he said, 'Your son has real talent. He should make a go of it if he works hard. It won't be much money to start with, but he'll be a man of the world when he's working.'

If Mrs Cluny had come to the clinic originally to fight for her son, she had received a victory far beyond her wildest aspirations, as she told Rolf McMaster many times in between sobs.

When they had left Antonia was alone with the consultant. 'That was brilliant,' she told him truthfully, and real admiration shone in her eyes.

'Just a happy set of circumstances that happened to come along together.' He sat down at his desk and stretched his arms above his head.

She thought he looked tired now as he said, 'It wasn't so very long ago that the vocation of most amputees was begging. True medical teamwork didn't start until the late nineteenth century. Now people believe, and rightly so, that a patient should get back into society. But that all depends on the attitude that an individual's happiness has some worth.'

And then, for no reason that she would like to

admit to herself, Antonia wanted this man to like her. It suddenly felt very important.

He surveyed her with half-sleepy, half-sensuous eyes. 'You played your part as a member of my team very well this morning. If my regular sister should ever be sick again, I'll ask especially for you.'

She felt pleased as she replied, 'Thank you, sir.' Then, 'You've finished your list of patients. Do you want me for anything else?'

He hid a slow smile behind his large hand. 'I can't seem to find my small goniometer. I've got some hand injuries to see this afternoon, and I'll need the small one to measure the delicate angles of movement in the fingers. Perhaps I left it in Reception.'

She found the small flat instrument on the working surface by the telephone, and as she turned out of Reception she heard a half-whispered call.

'Antonia, come here.'

It was Lindain, very smartly dressed in a beige suit and wearing his white coat. She walked towards him and into the outside corridor.

'I didn't think I'd see you here at McMaster's clinic,' he said. 'How have things gone? Has he guessed?'

She laughed up into his eyes. 'No, thank

goodness, he's still in the dark. Though I must admit I'd rather tell him and apologise.'

'No. . .' Lindain shook his head. 'This is much the best way. You know, there are some doctors who believe they walk on the right side of God. He's one of them. And he can be a right bastard in theatre if the show isn't being played exactly to his liking.'

'Well, he's been quite charming this morning.' She reached up to straighten out the collar of his white coat.

'As long as you keep him sweet, we'll be fine.'

'Are you coming to the flat for supper this evening?' she asked.

His response was slightly slow in coming. 'Not tonight, Antonia. A few of the medics and myself have got up a study group. It's an American idea, and really helpful when you're tired and you need to cram facts into your head. Another evening.'

As she walked back to Rolf McMaster's office she reflected that being a doctor's wife wouldn't be easy. But for Lindain she'd do anything.

Inside the office she was confronted by the consultant sitting on the front of his desk with his arms folded. 'Why was it necessary to seek a second opinion?' His tone was cutting.

Rolf McMaster's whole attitude was harsher and more abrupt than he would have used towards anyone else. But there was something about this staff nurse that tugged at his heart-strings. It wasn't just her beauty, it wasn't just her care and consideration for patients and their relatives, it was something indefinable that was affecting him. And he knew Lindain Smythe's antics. He wasn't about to let him use Antonia.

'I'm sorry. . . I don't understand,' she said.

'You're new to this hospital, but it hasn't taken you five minutes to find a young buck to caress. I will not tolerate open sexual behaviour in members of my staff!'

The accusation and callous delivery of his words stung her. She could not believe her ears. The wonderful doctor of a few minutes ago, who had displayed such mature clinical wisdom with patients, was now metamorphosing before her eyes. He was changing into that commanding man who had hijacked her.

'I don't know what you thought you saw,' she retorted. 'You must have been viewing the scene with a voyeur's eyes!'

His mouth was set in a vicious line, but she felt she was full of fiery emotion.

'I was straightening out my fiancé's lapel. We are. . .' She was about to say 'engaged', but corected herself and raced on, 'We are unoffi-cially engaged——'

Rolf McMaster threw back his head and

laughed cynically. ' "Unofficially engaged". . .is that what they call it nowadays.'

She could have hit him, her rage boiled up so much inside her.

'It's the truth. . .' she stammered.

As his black eyes bored into hers, he recognised her as the girl who had transported him to the Royal to operate on Eddy. Only moments ago he had wanted to protect her from Smythe, but she had lied straight-faced to him when he had asked if he'd met her before. His hurt now turned to mocking anger.

'Do you come from an acting family? I should think you do. Because, not hours previously, you gave a fine performance. I sincerely believed your portrayal of innocence.'

Antonia shuddered. She knew what was coming.

'You lied to me when I asked if we'd met before. You were that incompetent girl who argued and fussed when I needed to be here operating on a maimed young man.'

She hung her head, and found herself unable to speak.

He was raging on. 'Now I find you're a woman who has misinterpreted the essential qualities of a nurse. A good nurse should be warm and compassionate, not hot and passionate!'

'How dare you?' she shot back. 'I did my best

when you abducted my car. If you'd been a woman alone, and a stranger suddenly shot into your car, you'd be afraid. And you didn't exactly come across as reasoned and coherent when you were twittering on about your bird in your bonnet. I thought you were an escapee from the psychiatric ward!'

Her eyes met and held his. Her passions were roused, and she felt justified in defending herself.

Their eyes remained locked for some seconds. The short time seemed to go on for an eternity. He was burning into her soul, and she was afraid.

Then she thrust his goniometer at him. 'I don't believe you want me for anything else this morning, sir.' And she turned and fled.

CHAPTER THREE

ROLF MCMASTER's accusations had hit Antonia like a volley of automatic gunfire. Now, as she was taking TPRs on the ward, they still richocheted around inside her head.

Sister Cook had resumed her report of patients on the ward earlier that afternoon, and Antonia had felt slightly relieved to hear that Eddy had been given an above-knee amputation at a most suitable level. If the complications of infection did not set in, then there was a very good possibility that he would be able to be fitted with an adequate artificial limb.

She walked tentatively into the sun-room and on her left saw the patient who most occupied her thoughts. Eddy's bed was elevated at the end, his legs were protected by a cradle under the bedclothes. And she saw that he slept peacefully.

She was glad he was not awake for their first meeting. This gave her some time to come to terms with what she believed was her guilt. He was overweight and swarthy. It didn't look as though the muscles in his arms were used for anything more athletic than lifting pints of beer.

Antonia sighed audibly, knowing that the more physically fit a person was before an accident, the more chance they had of an uneventful recovery. Eddy, by the look of him, would have a long haul in front of him.

'So you're the new staff nurse! Someone told us that you were about fifty and looked like a battleaxe. There are some liars in this hospital!'

The laughing words broke into her stream of thoughts and she turned to face Michael Baxter.

He too had the end of his bed raised, but for lumbar traction. He had suffered a prolapsed intervertebral disc at the level of the fourth and fifth lumbar vertebrae. His grinning face looked up at hers. His backhanded compliment would have made her laugh in other circumstances. Now she suppressed her smile. 'Yes, I'm Staff Nurse Moore, and you're the ward joker, I presume, Michael.'

'That's one of my more enduring qualities.' He laughed rather too loudly for her liking.

'Shh. . .' She pointed to Eddy. Sleep was the best thing for him at the moment and she didn't want him to be woken suddenly.

Shaking down the mercury in the thermometer, she noticed that Michael was reading a heavy hardbacked book.

'What's this?'

He held up the cover, and she saw fabulous galactic monsters in an eerie outer space landscape.

'Sci-fi adventure,' he told her.

'Do grown men really read this stuff?' She looked more closely at the book, knowing that Michael was twenty-eight.

'A little of what you fantasy does you good,' he quipped.

She laughed. 'That's a dreadful play on words!'

'But I like it. And it's true.'

She popped the thermometer under his tongue and felt for his radial artery at his wrist. He was still smiling with his mouth closed when she retrieved the thermometer.

'Are you the new nurse?'

She turned suddenly to face Eddy. Her heart contracted as she looked into his eyes.

'Yes. How do you feel?' She saw his eyes were bleary.

He rubbed his face with podgy hands. 'Better for that nap. But I couldn't half do with a ciggy.'

'I don't think that's wise—not so soon after your anaesthetic.'

'Aw, let him have a smoke, Staff,' Michael butted in. 'Even a condemned man in front of a firing squad is entitled to a ciggy as a last request!'

Antonia glared at Michael. She felt his choice of words was inappropriate.

To her relief Eddy chuckled. 'True enough, I faced death, but I beat him. And I'm here to tell the tale.'

'And Eddy's a hero, Staff. Do you know he's an expert driver? He missed a little kiddy by inches.'

'I know,' she murmured.

'Here, have one of mine, pal.' A box of cigarettes flew through the air, landed on the frame of Eddy's leg cradle and slithered to the floor.

'Don't throw things like that!' Antonia was fierce because she felt over-protective towards Eddy. 'They could have hit his wound and caused a lot of pain!'

'Sorry, pal.' Michael looked at Eddy. 'I didn't mean anything.'

'Where there's no sense there's no feeling,' said Eddy, giggling.

Antonia bent to retrieve the box of cigarettes. Perhaps it was as well that Eddy could laugh about things. Although she wondered how long that reaction to his disability would last.

'Just a couple of puffs, Nurse,' said Eddy. 'Then I'll give them up for good—I know smoking isn't good for you.'

'Not good in any circumstances, really,' she agreed.

Michael wasn't helping matters. 'The matches are in the box,' he said.

Sister Cook's patient report had been sketchy. There hadn't been time for anything more than a quick overview. Antonia looked down the main ward to see if Sister was at her desk, but she wasn't. And there was no one else in sight to ask either.

'Have a heart, Nurse!' Eddy was speaking again. 'It'll be my last, honest. And I'll make it an occasion to remember. I'll blow a smoke ring for you.'

Antonia was hesitant. Would that do any real or lasting harm?

'I was down in Physio this morning,' Michael chipped in again. 'They had an asthmatic kid there and he was blowing bubbles. The physio said it was a good exercise for his lungs. Now, using that logic, blowing smoke rings is in the same category.'

Antonia repressed a laugh. She knew all this supposedly light-hearted banter was intended to sway her better judgement and make her give in to them.

'All right. But you'd better make it a perfect smoke ring. And in only five attempts.'

Five attempts turned into six and then seven.

'This really must be your last try, Eddy,' Antonia said. The sun-room was full of hazy smoke, and she turned to open a window. It was a hot sunny day and neither patient would be in a draught.

'Put that cigarette out!'

Instantly, Antonia recognised that voice, full of natural authority. Swivelling around, she saw Rolf McMaster standing over Eddy and offering an ashtray. How had he managed to creep up like that? He must have taken the ashtray from the top of Michael's locker. Things were stacking up badly against her.

Rolf McMaster's voice was firm as he spoke to his patient again. 'Eddy, don't you remember that I ordered you to give up tobacco this morning?'

'Yes.' Eddy looked dejected as he stubbed out the offending cigarette. It had burnt down almost to the filter.

The next reprove was aimed directly at Antonia. 'What can you have been thinking of, Staff Nurse? Surely you know the complications that can arise post-operatively?'

Before she could answer Eddy spoke up in her defence. 'It wasn't her fault, sir. I nagged her. I said I could blow a smoke ring.'

'We both pressured her, Mr McMaster. She

shouldn't take all the blame.' Now Michael came to her rescue.

The consultant's gaze swept over the two men and back to Antonia. 'Amazing! You do seem to inspire great feelings of loyalty in men that you can only have known for a few hours.'

She thought his tone superior, and she didn't like his insinuation. Inwardly she burned.

He spoke to Eddy again. 'Cigarettes are out for you, young man. If you're so keen to play these sort of games, I'll arrange for the physio to bring you a tub of soap bubbles. The physio gym was full of the things this morning. I thought I was in a soap-sud commercial!' Then, turning to Antonia, he said, 'I'd like to examine Eddy's leg.'

She galvanised herself for action, pulled the curtains and folded down his bedclothes. The cradle was a bit tricky to remove, as one part was under the mattress. Rolf McMaster helped her, and as their hands touched she drew hers away quickly.

Something else appeared to displease the consultant. 'You're not lying very straight in your bed. Your pelvis is a bit skew-whiff.'

'Is it?' Eddy looked down. 'I've got to keep it level. Now I remember.' He placed his thumbs on his iliac crests and hiked up his hip, at the same time adducting his amputated leg. 'That's more level, isn't it, sir?'

'Excellent,' Rolf McMaster replied. 'You've got a good memory when you want to use it. Just remember to check your pelvis periodically. We don't want you to develop an abduction contracture.'

He was referring to the abductor muscles that ran down the outside of the thigh. If these sectioned muscles did become over-short, then the leg would stick out to the side, and this would affect the way Eddy would walk in his prosthesis. Mr McMaster explained this again to his patient.

Antonia felt claustrophobic behind the curtains. She grew hot and ran her fingers across her brow as Rolf McMaster inspected the dressings.

Because Eddy had had a traumatic amputation the consultant had faced a potentially infected area at operation, and now Eddy's leg was encased in a soft dressing.

If the amputated part had been surgically clean then Eddy could have had a rigid plaster dressing, or better still an IPSPF—an immediate post-surgical prosthetic fitting—and then there would have been a very short time between surgery and the fitting of an articifial leg.

Antonia watched Rolf McMaster's gentle fingers palpate the skin directly proximal to the dressing.

'Hmm. . .everything looks reasonable. Have you had any increase in pain?'

'No.' Eddy shook his head. 'But. . .' He looked puzzled and embarrassed at the same time. 'I feel as if there's a funny pins and needles feeling in my big toe.'

The surgeon nodded. 'That's only natural. It's the phantom limb.'

'Phantom?' Eddy queried. 'Sounds like a ghost!'

'You're right. It's not all a figment of your imagination. It's a very odd thing, especially for you to feel, but some authorities think that the body image persists as an intact perception, even though you've actually lost the part.'

Antonia saw him watch Eddy intently for any adverse reaction. But there was none.

Mr McMaster continued, 'Yes, some patients think they're hallucinating when they feel the phantom. But it's been documented since 1551 by a French surgeon named Ambroise Paré.'

The name Paré made Antonia think of her first encounter with this surgeon. If only he hadn't been so covered in dust at the time! If only she had heard of Paré before.

'Let's see the chart, please, Staff.'

'I haven't taken the afternoon readings yet, Mr McMaster.'

'Too busy playing Red Indian games, I suppose. Try and remember that smoke signals as a means of communication aren't clinically acceptable on a hospital ward.'

She hated his disdainful eyes.

He spoke again. 'While you take the TPR I'll have a look at Michael.'

Antonia popped the thermometer into Eddy's mouth as he pulled a face. Then after remaking the bed and pulling back the curtains she felt for his pulse.

Rolf McMaster was only with Michael for a very short time, and while Antonia was taking the pulse count he came and stood beside her. His presence unnerved her, and she had to concentrate very hard to remember the pulse count and observe the chest movement to count respiration as well.

As she noted down the readings on the chart, Rolf McMaster gazed over her shoulder. 'Your temperature's slightly up, Eddy, but it's within normal limits.' Then to Antonia. 'I made the number of respirations per minute one less than you.'

She looked up at him aghast. Was he going to publicly reprimand her for this as well?

'But I'll let your count stand. It's acceptable.

And there's always some slight error when the measurements are done on the eye, so to speak.'

She exhaled gratefully.

'I'll have a word with you on the ward now.' And, saying good morning to the two patients, the consultant strode up the ward at a great pace.

Antonia caught up with him at Sister's desk, and wasn't in the least surprised that he sat in Sister's big swivel chair and indicated the smaller one for her to sit on.

As he leaned over the desk-top his grey eyes bored into hers. 'As a nurse on the ward you are the first line of defence against infection. Eddy is overweight—that won't help matters. But, more importantly, there is a history of diabetes in his family.'

Antonia lowered her eyelashes and bit her lip. 'I didn't know.'

'Then make it your business to know—you're his nurse. Diabetics don't heal well. As yet, we've found no confirmation of sugar in his urine. . .' He rubbed his index finger across his upper lip. 'Smoking is out, not only because of the possibility of delayed healing, but I don't want him to develop any sort of post-operative chest infection. I don't want him coughing and spluttering infected sputum all over his bed.'

Inwardly Antonia groaned. She felt even worse.

'And for God's sake, get his TPR recordings accurate. You know I can't inspect the wound at this early stage. Pulling the dressings off now might only cause an infection to be introduced. And TPRs and other clinical and lab findings are all I've got to guide me.'

'I'm sorry, sir.' Her voice was only just audible. She sat there staring down at the top of Sister's desk while tension mounted and silent seconds ticked by.

At last she could bear it no longer. She looked up, expecting to be confronted by a contemptuous face, but he only looked puzzled and somewhat concerned.

And his voice when he spoke was gentle. 'Antonia, starting a new job is a most difficult thing. Try to concentrate on all these new patients under your care, and all the new regimes that are so vital.'

She was holding her breath. His new approach was so stunning to her.

He continued, 'Don't be swayed by frivolous romantic notions. If you put your job first, you'll find your life is far less complicated.'

She couldn't believe how fatherly he sounded, even if she did resent his advice.

'And if you have any problems, consult me.'

Pushing on the desk with his hands and leaning slightly over towards her, he stood up and repeated softly, 'Consult me.'

He left the ward immediately, and Antonia sat as if rooted to the spot. How on earth could she consult him about her problems when he was the major one?

The week passed by without any major catastrophes on the ward. Antonia had the weekend off, and on Saturday afternoon she sat drinking orange juice in her flat.

She had hardly seen Lindain, his studies had kept him so preoccupied. But, even though he was on call this weekend, he had promised that he would try and get an hour or so off and visit her.

The doorbell chimed. 'It must be him,' she said aloud, and ran down the stairs to her door.

'Oh, no—Rupert! Who are you today?' she exclaimed. 'You look nearly normal.'

Rupert was Antonia's younger brother. He was studying fashion and design at a nearby university. She loved him dearly, but apart from his unusual outlandish costumes he had an irritating tendency to play outrageous pranks. And she wasn't in the mood for his frivolous side just now.

'What a way to greet a member of your family!

You don't deserve a visit or a house-warming present.' He kissed her and handed over a flat hard object wrapped in white velvet and tied with a white silk ribbon. 'And I'm a gangster of love today. That's why I'm wearing a black waistcoat,' he ran his hands down his chest, 'my black jeans, and my passionate pink bow-tie.' He pulled his bow-tie deftly.

Antonia stood back. 'Well, you might have looked more presentable if you'd worn a shirt, or even a T-shirt.'

'Nonsense! You've no style, Antonia. My client today was a young debutante. I've just measured her up for a ballgown. And she thought I looked quite splendid. . . And so did her mother.' He winked.

'How does Rosalind put up with you?' She laughed at him.

'Because we're a perfect match,' he said as he grinned back at her.

Rosalind was Rupert's fiancée. They were in the same classes at university, and had formed their own designer fashion business.

Antonia untied her present, and wasn't surprised to see that it was a pen and ink drawing framed in tortoiseshell.

'I don't know what came over me to draw that picture for you, Toni,' Rupert told her. 'We've been studying Max Ernst at school, so I suppose that accounts for the subject-matter.'

Antonia saw a scene with two people in an elegant period drawing-room. They were standing with their backs to a roaring fire. The young girl was dressed in a ballgown, and her companion was in full evening dress too. But, although he had the body of a human, he had the head and feathered fingers of a hawk. And he was looking at the girl with covetous eyes.

The picture sent a shiver down Antonia's spine. 'Lovely,' she said quietly.

'It takes a bit of getting used to,' Rupert said. 'But it'll grow on you. One of my professors was quite taken with it.'

Pity he didn't actually take it, thought Antonia. But she didn't want to appear rude, so she said nothing.

She showed her brother all over the flat. In the bedroom he said, 'Why haven't you hung up the curtains? Were they too high for you to reach?'

This wasn't the reason. Antonia had deliberately left them down, because more light filtered into her room at night without them.

'Yes. . .'

'I'll find a chair and hang them for you. Drapery is an art, you know, and I'll make a better job of it than anyone.'

She lay on the bed and watched him fastidiously arrange the folds.

'I suppose it would have been too much to expect Lindain to help you,' he remarked. 'He has to keep his hands for the more important things in life, like lifting champagne glasses and shaking the hands of consultants with due deference.'

'Why are you always so nasty to him?'

'I don't like him,' came the flat reply. 'You know, you'll be a very wealthy young woman in time, Toni. Dad's wealth was widely known, and it was splashed all over the newspapers. I bet Lindain's spoken to you about the will and your inheritance. I can't help thinking——'

She cut him short. 'Lindain's not marrying me for money. He's got enough of his own.'

'No amount would be enough. It would just burn holes in the pockets of those Savile Row suits of his.'

She looked away, sighed and closed her eyes.

Rupert climbed down from the chair and stood over her. 'You've got a new job, now get a new man in your life. Lindain's got no fun in him. He's got no buzz. I'm serious, Toni Ankle.'

How could she take anything her brother said seriously? Especially when he called her by that ridiculous name that he'd coined for her—Toe. . .knee. . .ankle.

She continued to stare away from him. There was certainly one man in her life with buzz. That was Rolf McMaster. And, in his case, buzz meant that he had a sting in his tail.

She didn't feel like an argument. Rupert would never change his mind. For some reason he was biased.

Sitting up, she looked into her brother's eyes. 'Why don't you ring your beloved Rosalind? Here's the phone.' She pointed it out on her bedside table.

'If you marry Lindain you'll have one hell of a life.'

'How about a mug of tea and some jam cream doughnuts?' She knew he loved them. 'I'll put the kettle on, and buy some fresh ones. They sell them two doors away.' She would hear nothing against Lindain.

Rupert agreed, but he sounded dispirited.

In the small kitchen Antonia plugged in the kettle. Laughter and soft seductive-sounding words filtered through to her. It was true, she and Lindain never seemed to have fun in their relationship.

For a split second she wondered if there was something lacking. But then again, no. Her brother and his fiancée were much younger. They were arty types. And everything about them was over the top and hyped up.

She had met Lindain shortly after her parents' death—sombre circumstances. And the two of them had dedicated jobs. There was no room for fun and games in their lives.

In the cake shop she had to wait in a long queue, then two neighbours cornered her, and it was some time before she could make her way home.

Climbing up the stairs, she heard raucous laughter, and the voices of two men. It must be Lindain and Rupert. At last her brother was making an effort to be nice.

Antonia's face was shining with delight as she entered the small kitchen.

'Hello——' Her words were cut short in her throat.

That dominant figure lounging at her kitchen table with a mug of tea in his hand wasn't Lindain. It was Mr Rolf McMaster.

CHAPTER FOUR

'HELLO, Toni Ankle.' Rolf's eyes were bright with amusement.

She could have cursed him outright for calling her that silly pet name that Rupert insisted on using. And she could have doubly cursed her brother for letting Rolf McMaster into her flat.

'Rolf's been telling me that you work together,' Rupert broke the silence, then sped on. 'You know, I've got to get back quickly and see Rosalind.' He stood up, and shook hands with Rolf. 'Bye—great to have met you. I want a word with Toni downstairs; you don't mind if I have her for a short while? Then she's all yours.' He half whispered this last sentence.

'Not at all.' Rolf sounded affable, but there was such a twinkle in his eyes that Antonia felt sure that something had been going on behind her back.

Once outside in the alley Antonia let fly. 'Why on earth did you let him in?'

Rupert assumed an astonished look. He took no notice of her question. 'That man really fancies you, Toni.'

'What rubbish! You don't know what you're talking about!'

'Oh, yes, I do. When I opened the door to him he looked at me with murderous eyes. The first thing I said was, "I'm her brother," then we were firm pals.'

She covered her eyes with her hands and groaned.

'He's got a great body, especially his torso,' Rupert continued. 'I told him that if he was ever hard up for cash, the arts department pays a good rate for nude models in the life sketching class.'

Antonia felt her cheeks burning red. 'You fool, Rupert! Mr McMaster doesn't need money. He's an orthopaedic consultant.'

'Oh, a doctor. I'm so glad. I thought he was a remedial gymnast, with muscles like those.'

'I'm going to die of shame and embarrassment!' She leant against Rupert's van. 'What have you been up to in that kitchen up there?'

'Nothing. . . I've never seen you so passionate, Toni. It suits you, go up straight away.'

'One day I'll kill you.' Her words were barely audible above his laughter.

'Rosalind wouldn't want to become a widow before she was married,' he quipped as he jumped into his van.

She was seething as he wound down his

window and whispered, 'Don't keep him waiting, he's probably between your sheets right now!'

'Goodbye, Rupert—come back when you're in a less interfering mood.' And bring Rosalind, I'll feel safer with another woman present, she thought.

When Rupert had gone she stood trembling at the bottom of her stairs. Her brother was capable of setting up the most outrageous pranks. And Rolf McMaster was. . .an unknown quantity. Why wasn't Lindain here to protect her?

She crept up the stairs, along the short landing, and looked into the kitchen. There was no one there.

She felt a quiver run through her heart. Rolf McMaster couldn't possibly be in the. . . The thought made her shiver.

Silently she peered into the lounge—empty. Gingerly, she pushed open the bathroom door—empty. There was only one more room left to inspect. Outside the bedroom door she hesitated.

'Are you looking for me?' A deep velvet voice behind her made her jump round.

'Where have you sprung from?'

'Your kitchen, of course. Where else?' He looked devilishly amused. 'Your kitchen table had a wobbly leg, so I adjusted its screw foot for you.'

She stared at him, not knowing what to say.

He was leaning on the door-jamb, completely filling the doorway with his bulk. Then he turned and without a word strolled back into the kitchen.

If Antonia wanted to have any sort of conversation with him, she was forced to follow. It was as if he were the master here.

After a moment or two during which she steadied her breathing and her nerves, she followed. He was standing by the window, holding Rupert's pen and ink sketch in his hands.

As she saw him intently looking at the figures in the picture she shrank inside. It made her acutely embarrassed. Somehow it was as if he was studying her. Her thoughts confused her.

'It's unusual to meet two brilliant artists who can make successful careers out of their talents,' he mused. 'Your brother's work is stunning.' He held the picture for her to see. 'It's as if the lines are vibrant and alive.'

She didn't want to look. It felt as if he were forcing her against her will.

He continued, 'I admire your brother. He has enterprise and determination, as well as being artistically gifted. His business should do well.'

Antonia hadn't been away from the flat for long, yet Rolf McMaster seemed to know a lot about her brother.

'I saw Hans Stein this morning,' he went on.

'Nigel Cluny got the job as goldsmith's apprentice. Hans was as impressed with Nigel's work as I was. So he'll start work as soon as school finishes.'

This brought Antonia back on to firmer ground. She remembered the short above-knee amputation vividly. 'That's wonderful! I bet he's over the moon.'

'He certainly was.' There was a short pause as Rolf McMaster put Rupert's pen and ink drawing up against the wall. 'Will you hang this here?'

'I don't think so.' She was wary of him again.

'In the bedroom, then. . .?'

'I'll think about it.' She approached boldly and took the picture from him. There was something about his smile she didn't trust.

'I've been thinking about you, Toni Ankle——'

'Don't call me that ridiculous name!'

'I like it. I think it suits you. After all, you're a staff nurse on an orthopaedic ward.'

'Only family call me that,' she replied stiffly. He was making her feel nervous again.

'I've been thinking about you, Toni. . . And I've come to apologise.'

This stunned her.

'When I hijacked you and your car the morning I had to operate on Eddy, I could think of nothing but getting to theatre quickly. I'm sorry if I frightened you.' His eyes were genuine. He carried on, 'And you were right, I must have sounded completely crazy, twittering on about my blackbird.'

An apology was the last thing she had expected to hear from him. 'The circumstances were very odd,' she conceded.

'So I've come to invite you to visit my family of blackbirds. I've consulted with the mother blackbird and she says she's open to visitors this afternoon.'

Antonia laughed. She suddenly felt a surge of relief. 'Then I'd be delighted to visit.'

Out in the back alley Rolf McMaster opened the car door for her and helped her in. It was a five-door Range Rover. Then she watched him climb gracefully in beside her. He was very agile for a big man.

'I bought this car immediately after our first. . .encounter,' he explained. And she felt very aware then that his apology over the hijack was sincere.

They drove a short distance up some back roads and then turned in through white gates. This was not the magnificent approach to the front of Hawksworth. Antonia saw a cobbled yard, and a black and white gabled red brick house.

'Is this where you live?' she asked tentatively.

'This used to be the stables. It's a garage now.'

Of course, Hawksworth must have had a garage, and when she looked to her left the back of the Gothic mansion loomed grey through the trees. So all her detective work on the day of their first meeting had been wrong.

Rolf held a finger across his lips as he helped her out of the Range Rover. 'Shh. . .! The nest is in my sports car, and it's very near the side door where we'll go in.'

Silently she followed him into the garage. It was lofty and cool inside. She saw the red sports car ahead. The bonnet was up and the engine was protected by an old worn carpet.

'What's that on the floor?' She detained him with a light touch on his forearm. Something dull pink lay on the ground only steps ahead of them. She knelt down. It was a nestling, and it was cold to her touch.

Antonia picked the inert creature up. 'Is it dead?'

'Give her to me. I'll warm her with my hands—they're bigger than yours.'

She watched as he enclosed the tiny body with his hands. Only the small head showed between his long fingers.

'There's a heartbeat all right.' Then after a moment, 'I think she must have fallen out of the nest just a few minutes ago. Her temperature's gaining rapidly, her core temperature can't have dropped much.'

In the half-light of the garage she saw his face etched in hard planes. But his voice and eyes were full of kindness.

The nestling began to struggle, and Antonia was delighted. 'Back to the nest for this young one now, I think,' he said.

As he made room for his charge in the nest shaped like a bulky cup he said, 'Look, you can see how she was jiggled out. It's a big clutch, five babies.'

She bent closer to inspect, but an alarm call, 'Pook! Pook!' made the young birds silent and motionless.

Antonia's eyes searched for the sound and she saw the mother blackbird perched high up on a window-sill. She was crouching low, and her head was down. Fierce black eyes assailed Antonia.

Rolf McMaster's hand encircled her bare arm. 'We're directly between mother and babies, and she doesn't know you.'

He pulled her to one side and into the shadowy area of the garage. 'Stand very still,' he whispered from behind and close to her ear. 'If she thinks you're a part of my silhouette she'll think you're no threat.'

Antonia felt his arms glide about her body. One hand came to rest low down on the flat of her stomach, and the other just below the fullness of her left breast.

Her heart began to hammer violently against the closeness of his physical touch. He must feel it, she thought.

In the seconds that elapsed, she felt suspended between reality and a magical sense. The bird still threatened her in front, but it was the man behind her, who held her so fast, who had captured her and now made her equilibrium shake.

'Keep breathing.' She heard him again, but as if through a mist a long way off.

If she breathed from her diaphragm her belly pressed into his one hand, and if she breathed from the sides of her rib-cage, his other hand was there. There was only the apex of her lungs left.

Fortunately the bird fluttered down to her brood and began feeding them with pieces of chopped-up worm nicely covered in earth.

'Our little one's taking food, she must be all right.' His voice was full of warmth.

Her body relaxed, then she felt him tighten his grip. The blackbird gave them a curious look over her shoulder.

Rolf McMaster spoke directly to the bird. 'It's OK, dark angel. This one belongs to me.'

Antonia felt an undeniable desire seep up through her body, licking fire through her veins. She flushed, and to her shame she knew Rolf McMaster was as aware of her reaction as she was.

Having surveyed the two humans with disarmingly knowing eyes, the bird flew back out of the window.

With an effort Antonia broke free of the consultant. She took a few steps towards the nest. 'Yes, they're all perfectly healthy-looking.'

He was close behind her again. 'We work well together, Toni. It's not every day that you have an experience like that.'

She was acutely aware of the maleness of her companion. His torso was magnificent, his thighs well sculpted beneath his blue jeans, and the musky scent of him made her quiver again.

Quickly she looked up and saw his eyes deeply dilated. They were dark and dangerous. And just as quickly she focused back on the nestlings.

'They're not afraid of us. . .'

'No.' He spoke slowly. 'They're under a week old.'

'They'll ruin the inside of your engine, even if you have put this old rug here for protection.' She couldn't bear to look into his eyes.

'I'll sell the sports car when they've no further use for it.' His voice was matter-of-fact. 'I don't feel the need for fast cars and driving in the fast lane any longer. In a way, the birds have done me a favour. I've got the Range Rover now, and it suits my purposes.'

She felt compelled to look at him.

A slow smile crossed his face. 'The mother blackbird gave you a very thorough once-over! But you seem to have passed inspection, otherwise she wouldn't have left her brood.'

'I'm glad I've seen the family.' She bent over the nestlings again, avoiding him. 'You must hear wonderful birdsong here.' She hardly knew what she was saying.

'It's a very fine dawn chorus, if you want to stay one night and hear it the next morning.'

'Oh. . .' He was confusing her more and more. 'I didn't mean. . .'

'You're a chaste young lady, Toni, I can see that.'

Did he have to bring everything around to a very personal level?

Then his eyebrows knitted together slightly. 'The dawn chorus is best. At this time of year you wouldn't want to hear a male blackbird singing persistently throughout the day.'

It was a strange thing to say. She wondered, as she watched his face. 'Why?' she asked.

It was as if an old and painful memory crossed his mind. 'Because he would have lost his mate, and he'd be singing to attract a female. And if he was lucky he'd find one before the season was ended.'

She stared at him.

'Come into the house, I'll show you around.'

Somehow she knew it was dangerous, but it was as if she was entirely under his control.

He led her through a courtyard area, decked out with white cast-aluminium garden furniture, and opened the french windows for her to enter Hawksworth.

The windows were tall, the upper two thirds of glass subdivided into squares by a wooden framework. They cast a squared pattern on the floor in the house.

The room that confronted her was vast. It stretched the whole length of the house. Heavy wooden dividing doors were folded back on their hinges. The whole area could be divided into two rooms.

It was unfurnished, except for two leather armchairs, a coffee-table and a huge mahogany bookcase that was situated against one cream wall next to the fireplace.

'It's a spartan set-up at the momnent. I haven't decided exactly how to furnish the place yet.' Then, looking down at her, he said, 'Would you like a cool drink, lemonade, orange juice?'

Her surroundings so impressed her, she answered, 'Orange juice, please, sir.'

His laugh was light. 'You call me Rolf. . . Wander around the house while I fix the drinks.'

She felt a little unreal in the large room that echoed her footsteps. There were only black stained boards on the floor.

The bookcase was taller than herself. Books of all sizes were crammed together. And in front of her, at exactly her eye level, she saw a beautiful brown leather book. It was embossed with gold leaf and intricate geometric designs. It bore a single word on its spine—PARÉ.

Here was a book all about Rolf's hero. She took it down to examine it more closely. Inside was a profile of the surgeon. Paré looked serious and he was dressed in the court clothes of his day. The book was a limited edition, number 783 of 1,900, a facsimile reprint of 1564. But— oh. . .all in French! She couldn't understand the gist of it.

She flicked through the thick parchment-like paper and came to a strange drawing—artificial limbs set in a landscape among birds, snails and what looked like a tortoise.

'So you've found my favourite book.' Rolf's voice was close behind her. He put down the tall glasses on the low table.

'Who exactly was Paré?'

Rolf spoke admiringly. 'Ambroise Paré was one of the most important men in medicine. He radically changed methods of treating wounds, especially for amputees. He reintroduced the ligature. And ligatures were set out by Hippocrates, but had fallen into disuse since the first century AD. An amputated limb was treated by immersion in boiling oil or by crushing.'

Antonia was revulsed. 'I can't believe ligatures weren't used for so many centuries.' She knew that it was an ingenious method of tying off a blood vessel without substantial loss of blood.

'That wasn't all that Paré did. Among other things, he founded orthopaedics. He worked with armourers to develop artificial limbs. In his work he describes a prosthesis for an above-knee amp with an adjustable socket and a controlled knee lock. These are principles still used today.'

'He must have had a fantastic mind.'

Rolf smiled and shook his head. 'He came to Paris as a rustic barber's apprentice when he was only nineteen, and received some training as a dresser at the Hôtel-Dieu. He worked on the battlefields and then worked his way up to become surgeon to the King of France.'

He took the book from her hands. 'There are more fascinating drawings.' He showed her strange devices for making the instruments sterile, then a page with surgical instruments. 'Look at this saw, there's a lion's head on the end of the handle.'

'And a ring through its mouth!' She was fascinated.

'And here. . .' Rolf pointed out a scalpel. 'It folds into the handle like a pocket-knife.'

'And there's a tiny winged female on the handle.' Antonia screwed up her eyes to focus more closely.

As she was studying the elegantly worked angel, Rolf spoke in a deep slow voice. 'She's beautiful but not living. She would be hard and cool to the touch. Not like. . .' He took the book from Antonia's hands, placed it back on the shelf and stared steadfastly into her eyes. 'Not like. . .a real woman.'

His fingertips tilted her chin up. She was forced to look directly into those mysterious, shining eyes. They were dilated again, but they shone with light. They were mesmeric.

Firm warm lips came down on hers, and she shuddered as sensation upon sensation radiated through her entire body.

His hands closed around hers and brought them to rest behind his neck. 'I didn't mean this to happen so swiftly.' His voice was husky. He kissed her more deeply, probing her mouth, delighting her even more.

Was it the heady scent of the roses that filled

the room? Was it the hazy heat of the hot summer afternoon? Her sense of self-control was slipping away. She kissed him back, standing on tiptoe to be closer.

His hands swept around her waist, pressing into the hollow of her back, then down over her bottom, so that he could pull her even closer against his hard masculine body.

She was filled with physical want. At that moment she desired no one else in the world.

She had been standing in a cage of light and dark shadow thrown on to the ground by the french windows. Now he pulled her on to one of the armchairs that was flooded with warm sunshine. She clung to him as his breathing became ragged. His hands slid around her leg, pushing her thighs apart as his kiss probed even deeper.

'Wherever you are, darling, come and give me a hand with all this shopping!' A young woman's voice rang out as clear and as beautiful as a church bell.

Antonia's eyes flew open. Whatever had come over her? Whatever was she doing on this man's lap?

Rolf looked bright and very pleased. 'It's Kay. She's a dear and very old friend, Toni.'

Antonia scrambled to stand alone. Rolf's arm was about her waist. 'Stay here a moment, then I'll bring her in and introduce you. I want you to be good friends.' He looked at her tenderly, then mischievously. 'I'd better let my body cool down!'

She was confused by his words, and embarrassed by her actions. Her cheeks were hot and burning like the rest of her body.

Her mind began to clear. She must have been insane to have let such a thing happen! She could hear muffled voices, and tentatively she stepped towards the door that led to the hall.

Mirrors were stacked higgledy-piggledy on the floor, leaning against the wall. She saw Rolf and the other woman's reflection quite clearly. Their conversation was only just distinct.

'Darling Rolf, how wonderful.' The woman caressed his cheek with her palm. 'It's about time the two of us had someone new in our lives.'

Then Antonia saw Rolf take her hand and kiss it.

He had called the blackbird his dark angel only moments ago, and in that same breath said that Antonia had belonged to him. Now he had yet another woman with dark hair. How many dark angels did this man need?

Before she could make her escape Antonia was confronted with Rolf and the dark-haired beauty. And beautiful she was, with brilliant brown eyes, long dark wavy hair and a flawless complexion.

'Antonia Moore, this is Kay Warner,' said Rolf.

The woman held out an elegant hand. 'I'm so pleased to meet you. Rolf keeps many things close to his heart.' Her eyes looked warm. It was as if she had said, 'And I'm glad you're one of them.'

Antonia was covered in confusion. Did Rolf and this woman share what some people called an 'open relationship'? So open that they could make love to whoever else they pleased. If this was true, she had no intention of being part of a ménage à trois.

Kay spoke again. 'You'll stay for tea, of course?'

Struggling to appear coherent in this bizarre scene, Antonia only managed to say, 'I'm glad to have met you, but I'm afraid I can't stay. I'm needed at home.'

The other woman looked curiously perplexed. 'I'll go and put your frozen food in the freezer, Rolf. You persuade Antonia to stay.' Then, to Antonia, 'He can be very persuasive, I know.'

This was too much. Antonia headed for the front door, which was still ajar. She didn't want to have anything more to do with Rolf McMaster.

On the front steps he caught hold of her arm. 'Toni, you don't understand. Kay is an old friend, that's all. We've known each other for years, ever since——'

Her breathing was rapid now, her breasts rising and falling quickly. 'I have to be home to make Lindain's tea——'

'Dr Lindain Smythe!' Rolf was incensed at hearing the name. 'How does that man have time to fit you into his schedule? He's got a Casanova complex, and he works it out on every available and willing woman in the hospital.'

Antonia was shocked. She felt like hitting him.

Rolf's voice was full of disdain, and his mouth was twisted into an ugly line. 'You call yourself his "unofficial fiancée". Well, I can tell you there are many in the hospital who think they go by the same name!'

Her eyes sparked electric blue. 'How dare you detract from another man's character? Just because you have a sudden surge of hormones with me, and I don't choose to respond——'

Rolf's eyes flashed directly into hers. The intensity almost physically hurt her. 'No, Antonia. . .you aren't reading your physiology correctly. In the garage and again in the drawing-room, your hormones were very nicely on the swell.'

Her breath caught in her throat and she felt a flood of scarlet shame stain her cheeks. 'I need some fresh air, Mr McMaster.' And with that she almost ran down the front drive and out through the entrance.

She was appalled at what had happened. She must never be alone with Rolf McMaster. She must never ever set foot in Hawksworth again.

CHAPTER FIVE

'MICHAEL came to Eddy's aid last night by throwing a jug of liquid over him.'

Sister Cook was giving the early morning report on Wednesday. Antonia and all the other nursing staff stood in the middle of the big ward in front of Sister's desk.

Not another nightmare, Antonia sighed to herself.

As if in answer Sister said, 'Yes, I'm afraid these nightmares of Eddy's are becoming too frequent for my liking. But he's still retaining his sense of humour—some of the time. When I went to see him this morning my foot stuck on a sticky patch on the floor, and both Eddy and Michael thought that hilarious. You see, Michael's jug wasn't filled with water, but orange juice.'

A young trainee nurse laughed and said, 'Michael's clever. That's his imagination for you!'

Antonia added, 'It must be from reading all those sci-fi books.'

There was more general laughter, most of it

hollow. Antonia wanted to know if Eddy dreamed about his accident.

'No.' Sister looked grave. 'He dreams about losing his remaining leg. It's a frequent thing with these traumatic amputees.'

There was a short silence before Sister continued, 'Although we should all be as gentle and compassionate with Eddy as we can, we must stand firm about some things.'

Antonia had noticed an increasing defiance in Eddy since the weekend. It was a reaction against his injury.

Sister was adamant. 'Miss Robinson, the physiotherapist, says he is determined to walk on his crutches alone now. But he's not ready— he's far too wobbly. On the ward he's only to walk with a nurse by his side, and a walking-belt around his waist. Is that clear?'

Everyone agreed. If Eddy fell and knocked his amputated leg, the wound might burst open.

Sister continued, 'I can understand that he's very anxious this morning. Today at eleven o'clock Mr McMaster will inspect his wound for the first time. His future treatment will depend on how well his tissues have healed.' She looked directly at Antonia. 'Staff Nurse, you'll assist Mr McMaster with this inspection, please.'

'Of course, Sister.' Antonia had anticipated this. Since the weekend she had successfully avoided the consultant. Their meeting would be an embarrassment, but she would have to go through with it for Eddy's sake.

When report had finished Antonia wheeled the wash trolley into the sun-room.

'At last!' cried Eddy. 'Night staff didn't give me a thorough wash, and I've still got a sticky area on my back.' Black circles under his eyes betrayed the ravages of the night.'

'Pity Michael doesn't drink spring water,' she said, smiling.

Eddy sniffed and became serious. 'Michael's a good mate. Aren't you, Michael?'

'Sure I am, when I need to get my beauty sleep too.' Michael's tone was deliberately light. 'He was thrashing about so much, Staff, I thought he'd fall out of bed. He couldn't wake up.'

'Yeah, you did me a good turn there,' Eddy told him. 'I woke up before the really bad part of that dream.'

'Hasn't Mr McMaster written you up a prescription to help you sleep?' Antonia was sure he had.

'Yes. But he said I was only to take the tablets if I thought I needed them. I think I'll have one tonight.'

As Antonia washed Eddy, Michael carried on talking even though he was brushing his teeth.

His disembodied voice penetrated through the curtain around Eddy's bed.

'This might be a good day for you and me, Eddy. Mr McMaster's going to examine me in Physio this morning, after I've had my intermittent traction on the machine. I might be free of this damn bed traction then, and go on the tilt table in Physio.'

'What's a tilt table?' Eddie wanted to know.

Antonia explained, 'When you've been lying flat on your back for weeks you get dizzy when you first attempt to stand.'

'That's it.' Michael took up the thread. 'I lie on a table with a board under my feet, then they tilt it up by degrees.'

'Yeah, then Mr McMaster's going to see me. He's going to take all the dressings off today. I bet I get a new leg soon.' The way Eddy said this revealed that he'd be one very disappointed man if this wasn't the case.

'I'll keep my fingers crossed for both of you,' Antonia added encouragingly.

Eddy asked where the dressings would be removed, and she told him that it would take place in the dressings-room just off the main ward.

'Will you be there?' Eddy looked at her very seriously.

'Yes.'

'Then I won't worry so much.' He looked slightly relieved.

When Antonia had finished her quota of bed-baths she returned to the sun-room to change the superficial part of Eddy's dressing. Michael had left the ward for his appointment in Physio.

What Antonia saw made her speak sharply. 'What on earth are you doing, Eddy?' Her concern for his recovery coupled with her perceived guilt often made her sound harsh, although in reality this was far from the truth.

He was on his crutches leaning over Michael's locker and peering at the sci-fi books. 'Thought I'd read for a bit.' As he turned he overbalanced slightly, and only saved himself by knocking hard up against Michael's bed.

Antonia shot round and grabbed him. 'You stupid lad!' she scolded. 'You know you shouldn't walk alone. Why didn't you use your wheelchair?'

'Keep your hair on, Staff!' He was full of indignation. 'They say you've got to practise before you're perfect.'

'Don't you dare do this again! Always call a nurse for help.' She was afraid he would fall.

He was really put out by her sharp tone. 'There's no need to speak like that.'

'There's every need. If you fall and your

wound breaks open, it'll take a darn sight longer to heal.'

Eddy was chastened and looked hard at the floor. Antonia saw he hated being dependent. She slipped her arm about his waist and held on to his pyjama jacket, while he walked back to his bed in stony silence.

'It's good advice,' she said softly as he lay back down on his bed.

'Yeah. OK.'

She pulled the dressings trolley close and screened his bed. 'Let's change this outer dressing.'

He was very withdrawn as she removed the compressive dressing of elastic wrap applied in the usual figure-of-eight manner. From behind her mask she said, 'As far as I can see, there hasn't been any more oozing of blood or fluid.'

'Does that mean everything's all right under the post-op dressing?'

He sounded so anxiously pathetic that she was sorry she'd been harsh with him earlier. But she knew she had had to take that line.

'It's difficult to say. We'll know more when Mr McMaster removes the conventional dressing of sterile gauze and fluff.'

'Can't you look now?'

Antonia was adamant. 'No, I can't remove that dressing. But if there was a raging infection in your wound, then we'd be able to smell a pretty foul odour by now, and it's not like that.'

Eddy's features relaxed as she told him this. But Antonia and all the staff knew another factor. Eddy's temperature had remained obstinately high since his admission—only by a small amount, but it might prove to be significant. She said nothing of this to her patient, because she hoped the negative sign was not due to pus.

As she applied the new dressing she was particularly careful to do so correctly, including Eddy in the procedure. 'Is the pressure of the bandage slightly more here?' She pointed to the lower end of his leg. 'Or here?' She indicated the upper part of the bandage near the groin.

He considered things and moved his leg tentatively. 'It's fine. There's slightly more pressure near the end.'

They had gone through this procedure many times. One day Eddy would have to bandage his own leg, and if he applied it with a restriction high up, then the stump would develop a pear shape and would be very difficult to fit into the socket of a prosthesis.

When they had finished it was time for Eddy's morning physio session. He was wheeled away by a porter, but not before Antonia had to issue another instruction.

'Try and remember not to sit with your leg

crossed over the other.' He had his amputated leg over his good one.

'Sorry, Staff, I just wasn't thinking.'

Antonia had dinned it into his head many times that sitting in that posture would only cause a flexion contracture to develop at his hip. At times like these she almost despaired. He couldn't seem to keep more than one instruction in his head at a time. What was he going to be like when he was discharged home?

There was a surprise waiting for Antonia in the canteen. Lindain sat alone at a table. She set her cup of coffee beside him and kissed him lightly on the cheek.

'At last we're together! It's been so long—over a week.'

He was taken aback momentarily when he saw her, and swiftly leaned his elbow on the table, covering his face with his wide-spread fingers. Really, he was peering through them to see who was in the area.

'Wonderful to see you too, darling. It's this terrible load of study that keeps me away from you.'

Lindain was confident that Antonia would understand this line. He also knew her loyalty was unswerving, and he deliberately played on this. During the short time they had worked apart he had enjoyed many a fling with a willing nurse, and he didn't relish losing his sexual freedom now. It was beginning to cramp his style having Antonia in the same hospital; he hadn't anticipated this. And he could run into her at any time or place. Now this began to make him edgy.

Antonia sighed. 'It isn't as if we're ships in the night passing each other. I don't see you then either.'

'What would be the point?' His face was suddenly sulky, like a little boy's. 'Your ridiculous old-fashioned prudery gets in the way.'

Her warm bright face clouded. He was bringing up that old problem of sex again. And she had made it clear that she wanted to be a virgin on her wedding night. His words embarrassed her.

They were silent for a moment, then she asked, 'How's work?'

'Not bad. At least McMaster's kept off my back since the weekend. They say it's because he's got a lady in his life. Somebody said he was thinking of marriage.'

Antonia's mind flashed back to Saturday. 'I don't doubt it. She's certainly very beautiful.' She was hardly thinking what she was saying. 'I saw her at Hawksworth.'

Lindain's face flashed astonishment. 'When were you there?'

She had let the cat out of the bag. 'On Saturday——'

'Why were you there?'

Antonia had to think fast. She could not reveal the whole sequence of events. Even a part of her now admitted that she had been under Rolf McMaster's spell, and she felt as if she had betrayed Lindain.

'He remembered who I was, and he came to the flat, apologised for frightening me when he commandeered my car, and took me to see his blackbird family.'

Lindain exhaled in relief. 'Well, I'm damned! Well done, Antonia! And I thought there was going to be trouble for me after that incident.' His face was excited. 'If he asks you again, tell him I'll come too. Yes. . .that could be very useful.'

Inwardly she groaned. She didn't want to go back to Hawksworth, either alone or with Lindain as chaperon.

'You see, McMaster has lots of old professor pals,' Lindain went on. 'And I'm sure two of them are going to examine me. . . Now if I'm well in with McMaster he can put a good word in for me.'

Antonia doubted that anything like that was

at all possible with Rolf McMaster. And secretly she began to despise Lindain a little. His shining armour was tarnishing.

Lindain was still jubilant. 'You've been such a good girl, I'll take you to the hospital Summer Ball.' He leaned closer. 'Nothing, not even study, will stop us.'

She was delighted. He was more like his old self. 'It's fancy dress, isn't it? Who shall we dress up as?'

Immediately he pooh-poohed the idea. 'Oh, no! We can't behave childishly like that. That sort of thing's for paramedics and junior doctors, and we must fit in with the consultants. I know McMaster's going, and he'll be wearing a formal evening suit—I overheard him say so.' He patted her hand. 'Keep that consultant sweet for me, there's a good girl. And don't make any slip-ups on the ward. He has a biting temper.'

Antonia remembered the upcoming removal of Eddy's dressing. Perhaps if she made some intelligent remarks about treatment, Rolf McMaster would see her as a nurse only, and then at the Ball he would know for sure that she belonged to Lindain.

'Phantom limb is fascinating,' she said. 'Do you know anything about it?' She told him that she'd like some information on the subject, so that she could answer intelligently if Rolf McMaster should ask her any questions.

'It's all in the patient's head.' Lindain sounded offhand. 'Some people have inadequate personalities, and after the injury—well, they're just plain loco. You know some insist on having the amputated limb buried. Then if it's raining on the "grave" they say they can feel their limb get wet,' he scoffed.

Antonia didn't feel this information was the sort of thing Rolf McMaster would welcome. He seemed to have a great empathy with his amputees.

Lindain continued, 'Don't worry about the amputees, Antonia. Modern technology is so advanced, they're almost as good as new when they get the new limbs. The stump's concealed, and if they make a bit of an effort with their exercise no one can tell.'

He told her he'd see her again, and as soon as he could, and as he walked away Antonia felt inwardly pained. Their relationship just wasn't the same. Rolf McMaster seemed to dominate everything around her, and he had succeeded in intruding very definitely into her personal life.

Looking at her fob watch gave her a start. It was time to get Eddy prepared for his big inspection. She knew her patient would have butterflies in his stomach over the procedure. But she had them too.

As Antonia was wheeling Eddy towards the dressings-room, Sister Cook called, 'Oh, Staff, Mr McMaster would like all the dressings and bandages left intact, so that he can see them.'

All the dressings, thought Antonia. He must want to inspect how well I do my job. But she had always done her best, especially with the bandaging. There was nothing faulty with her technique.

Eddy and Antonia entered through the pre-dressings area and then into the dressings-room proper. She noticed how trembly and sweaty Eddy was becoming. He was getting very nervous about the occasion.

She helped him on to the plinth, and put the back-rest only halfway up. That way, if he didn't want to look at the wound he could stare at the ceiling instead. After reassuring him that the procedure wasn't likely to be painful she set about preparing the sterile trolleys.

Everything was neatly ready when she saw a familiar dark head through the porthole of the connecting door.

'Here's Mr McMaster now, Eddy,' she told him. 'You'll soon have the verdict.'

He nodded and beads of perspiration trickled

down his forehead. She handed him some paper tissues.

A gowned and masked consultant strode in to greet them. 'Hello, Eddy. . . Ah, I see we've got Staff Nurse Moore to assist. That's good.' His eyes were full of reassurance for the patient and something like sparkles for Antonia.

She had wondered what sort of mood Rolf would be in when they next met. Their parting outside Hawksworth hadn't exactly been harmonious.

'That's a tidy bandage, Eddy.' The consultant inspected Antonia's handiwork. 'Who did it?'

Eddy replied, 'Staff Nurse here, mostly. She did this one this morning.'

Antonia was relieved that she had passed inspection so far.

All sterile procedures were rigidly adhered to during the removal of the soft dressing. 'Hmm. . .now we're coming to the nitty-gritty.' Rolf was very gentle as he removed the original post-operative material of sterile gauze and fluff.

Eddy looked steadfastly at the ceiling. Antonia knew that he would be shocked at first seeing his naked stump. Many patients were revolted.

Probing the area gently, Rolf said, 'That all looks very healthy. Good. . . I'm pleased.'

Eddy's sigh of relief was audible. He looked at

his stump and was silent. Then, 'Does that mean I can have a new leg now?'

'Hold on, young man!' Rolf's voice was soft but firm. 'The healing is good so far, but your leg isn't at a stage where it can tolerate a limb. I want the best for you, and I hope we'll be able to fit a total-contact socket.'

Eddy's face was crestfallen. 'But I thought I took weight through a bone in my pelvis. That's what they said in Physio.'

'That's true. Let me put a fresh dressing on your wound and then I'll explain about the limb and how your body copes with it.'

Rolf did the whole dressing himself, even the figure-of-eight bandage and the suspenders. Then he peeled off his gloves, threw them in the disposable bin and turned back to Eddy.

'When you have the new limb you'll virtually sit in the socket.' He pulled down his mask. 'The bone that will take the pressure is called your ischial tuberosity. It's at the back of your pelvis and it's the bone you take weight through when you sit.'

Eddy didn't look as though this was making much sense to him. His face was blank.

'It's unfortunate I haven't got a skeleton here to demonstrate.' Rolf's eyes caught Antonia's.

Surely he wasn't going to demonstrate that part of anatomy on her for Eddy's benefit? For an awkward moment she saw a wicked twinkle in his eye. This would be taking patient care too far, and Rolf would enjoy the experience too much.

To Antonia's relief, he undid the lower fastenings of his barrier gown and demonstrated the ischial tuberosity on himself. 'Right up here,' he told Eddy as he pushed his fingertips under the muscle on one side of his bottom.

He certainly had a magnificent physique, she thought. And he loved showing it off! She was glad when that demonstration was over.

Eddy seemed to understand about the socket fitting after a little more explanation.

'Your leg is a good shape to fit the prosthesis.' Rolf spoke encouragingly. 'That's because the bandaging has been excellently carried out.'

'Yes, I have to help do it now, and later I'll have to do it all by myself.' Eddy fingered one suspender.

Rolf continued, 'Do you understand about the varying pressure when you apply the bandage?'

'Um. . .yes. . .the pressure has to be more at the end of my leg. It's not got to be tighter at the top, otherwise I'll end up with a leg the shape of a fat lady's bum.'

The consultant threw back his head and roared with laughter. 'That's a very graphic description! We usually say pear-shaped. But your phrase is very apt.' He looked at Antonia with mock-serious eyes. 'Really, Staff Nurse Moore, where did you get such an expression from? Was one of your Sister Tutor's great aims to be a music-hall comedienne and tell gags at night?'

Antonia was aghast. She couldn't tell if the consultant was joking now or not. 'No, sir. And I don't know where Eddy got that expression from. Certainly not me.'

Eddy spoke up quickly. 'No, sir, it wasn't Staff here. The words just came into my head.'

The brightness returned to Rolf's eyes and his smile was wide. 'It's a good phrase—I'll use it when I'm lecturing. Sometimes those students are half asleep, even when I'm on the rostrum, and that'll certainly wake them up and make them take notice.'

Eddy had been looking slightly ill at ease, but he was more relaxed now. Rolf put his hand on his shoulder and said, 'Let me have a few words with Staff about your future dressings and then she'll take you back to your bed.'

In the pre-dressings room Rolf looked impressed. 'You've done a good job with Eddy. He's coming out of his trauma better than I expected. Lady Luck didn't deal him a good life card, but I think our good team approach will see him through.'

Antonia sighed. 'I'm so glad, sir.'

'Rolf. . .remember?' He placed his hand lightly on her forearm, and her heart contracted. His silky masculine magic was working on her again.

'He'll have had a shock just now, seeing his leg and the wound. I noticed he only took one glance, but that'll have been enough. Now, I want him to do something for the next half-hour or so. If he doesn't he may brood. It's very common for patients to feel deformed at this stage.'

Rolf squeezed her forearm, then thrust his hands in his trouser pockets. 'Take him back to the ward now, Toni. Lower his bed so it's horizontal and make him lie prone until lunch comes. That way, although he's only doing a passive stretch of his hip flexor muscles, he'll be doing something active out of his rehabilitation programme.'

She loved his concern and his warm eyes as he talked about his patient like this. And she told herself that the flutter in her heart was only due to her admiration of Rolf as a doctor.

'I'm glad that's all over,' Eddy said as Antonia helped him into his wheelchair.

As they passed through the pre-dressings area Antonia said, 'Oh, Eddy, please try and remember not to cross your stump over your good leg.'

'Sorry. . . I forgot.'

She bent closer to her patient as she pushed him out into the corridor. 'Don't worry about a thing. With modern technology, they'll make such a good leg, you'll be almost as good as new.'

She spoke to Eddy quietly, and if anyone could have overheard her they had to be the sort of person with exceptionally acute hearing.

In the sun-room Eddy's first words were, 'Oh, no, mate, you're still tied up to your traction.'

Antonia saw Michael looking very miserable.

'I didn't pass my tests.' Michael spoke slowly. 'McMaster found muscle weakness and a patch of anaesthesia on my leg, so I never made it to the tilt table.'

Eddy and Antonia were both sorry to hear this.

'How about you?' Michael craned his head round to get a better look at Eddy.

'They took the dressing off and it was all right. Course, Staff being with me made it a whole lot easier.' He turned to grin at her. 'Thanks.'

Eddy was easy to lay prone. He didn't make his usual complaints about it being difficult and uncomfortable.

As Antonia re-entered the pre-dressings-room to tidy up, she was unexpectedly confronted by a very hostile pair of grey eyes.

'It seems that it only takes you a few seconds to destroy nearly all the hard work of my rehab team on that patient! Think before you speak, Toni.'

Rolf's tone was so harsh that she almost stumbled in her tracks. Grey glinting eyes bore down on her and he moved closer.

'Don't ever refer to a patient's amputated limb as a "stump" in his presence.' His eyes flared fire. 'That's an ugly word, conjuring up mental images of hacked-down trees.'

Antonia almost cried out loud. Had she really used the word 'stump' to Eddy?

'When speaking to an amp say, "May I see your leg?" or "May I see your arm?" Do I make myself clear?'

'Yes, sir. . .' Her voice trailed away. Without looking up she could tell he was still livid. She could hear his rapid shallow breathing.

The problem had arisen because in her training Antonia had been taught to use the offending word to patients. No one but Rolf McMaster was so particularly concerned about patients' feelings.

But the fault lay squarely on her shoulders. Sister had told her not to use the word to Eddy's face, and she was sure that this morning was the only time she had slipped up.

'And the second major blunder. . .' His voice

rose again in admonishment. 'The second major blunder was to tell that poor lad that with a new limb he'd be almost as good as new.'

What was wrong with that? Antonia couldn't understand. But she continued to avoid Rolf's face.

'When a patient hears the phrase, "almost as good as new", he inevitably forgets the word "almost" and then thinks he's going to be as fit as his pre-accident level.'

She glanced up at him, then quickly away again. It seemed she had really done great harm, even if it had been unintentional.

Rolf kept hammering home his points. 'No artificial limb is as good as a natural one—they never can be. They're always uncomfortable, and they'll always require great effort on the part of the patient to use them.'

She covered her forehead with one hand.

'Now, if Eddy should have this idea of being a bionic man in his head, he'll feel he's failing when he doesn't reach that level of performance.'

She sobbed openly. 'I would never mean to hurt him. Never!'

Hostility hung in the air between them. It was tangible and devastatingly depressive to Antonia.

She felt her shoulders being gripped. 'I know you don't mean to hurt Eddy.' Rolf's tone was a shade warmer now. 'But you must concentrate when you're treating my patients.'

The silence stole up between them again. She was only aware of the tightness of his grip on her.

'I'm very disappointed in you, Toni—very disappointed. I was sure there was more to you.'

She looked up questioningly, and her vision began to blur as the tears welled up again.

Rolf produced a pocket handkerchief. 'Wipe your eyes.'

If she could have seen, she would have been surprised to see the look of pained concern on his face.

'Just don't use the word "stump" again like that, Toni, and when I think Eddy's in a psychologically fit state, I'll have a personal chat with him about the limitations of modern prosthetics.'

She wiped her eyes. 'I'm sorry,' she mumbled.

He was still gripping her shoulders. 'Come out to supper with me tonight. I can explain a lot of things about amputees then. I'm sure you'll learn a lot. . . And we can have fun learning in a more relaxed atmosphere.'

Suddenly she became wary. His tone had become caressive. What sort of fun happened in a relaxed atmosphere? Wasn't the beautiful Kay available tonight?

A wave of anger made her brush his hands

away. 'Dr Lindain Smythe and I are studying together tonight. I'll do all my personal learning with him, thank you.'

'That idiot Smythe again! Why don't you open your ears and eyes, Toni?' He was cold with disdain and his lip curled contemptuously.

She looked up at him, fiercely meeting his challenge.

Rolf took his handkerchief and stuffed it into his breast pocket. 'If you choose to learn from Smythe, then that's your prerogative. But for the sake of all the unfortunate patients who have to suffer contact with you. . .keep your mind on your textbooks and not on each other's anatomy!'

He left abruptly, slamming the door. The wooden frame vibrated a protest, and so did Antonia's whole body.

Now she remembered where the damning phrase, 'almost as good as new' had come from. Lindain.

The consultant and the anaesthetist were causing her great emotional upheaval. Her life would be far less complicated without either of them. She determined to cope alone.

CHAPTER SIX

IF ANTONIA thought she could cope alone, she was wrong.

On Thursday afternoon the porters were so busy that they hadn't the time to bring Eddy back from Physio. Sister asked for a volunteer, and Antonia went to fetch her patient.

Unusually, the physio department was situated in the basement of the Royal. She knew Eddy's afternoon session was in the weights-room, so she headed straight through Reception and past the individual treatment cubicles.

But Eddy was in the little gym with the high mats. He was watching a young man on the parallel bars.

'Found you at last!' Antonia walked round to hold on to the handles of his wheelchair. 'Ready for tea?'

'Yeah, I'm ready.' His face was very serious. 'Can we watch for a bit longer, though?'

'Of course.'

Antonia knew that seeing other amputees going through their paces would be a help to Eddy. The young man on the parallel bars was a double amp. He was wearing one above-knee and one below-knee prosthesis, and he was standing on two scales practising weight transference from one leg to the other.

'As soon as I've got my leg I'll be doing that.' Eddy sounded determined.

Antonia reached down to pat his shoulder. 'You'll have an easier time than him.' She kept her voice low. 'Double amps require far more balance training.'

The little gym only had two very small hopper-type windows, and even today no sunlight penetrated because a large van was parked outside, obscuring the light.

'It's coconut cake for tea,' Antonia coaxed, knowing this was Eddy's favourite.

'Great!' He grinned up at her, and then sat back in the wheelchair as she pushed him along.

Then it happened, the situation guaranteed to produce most fear in Antonia. And it was happening in a place where she always believed she would be safe. The whole physio department was suddenly plunged into total darkness.

She stopped dead in her tracks. A great wave of terrifying alarm built up inside her. She was enveloped in a fear so strong she believed she would die.

To Antonia the darkness was an overwhelming external threat, and her primal response of panic went into overdrive.

Her heart beat wildly against her rib-cage, her chest felt constricted and she was short of breath. She could see nothing but blackness, and ice-cold beads of sweat broke out on her face.

A feeling of faintness robbed her body of its usual strength and she gripped the handles of the wheelchair for support.

The whole reaction began to build into nightmare proportions. She was reliving the time down the mine—the time when the explosion had gone haywire and the young man had died in front of her.

She tried to stop the images of the past pressing down on her present. But they were uncontrollable. She could not stop them. Struggling to regain control, she tried to concentrate, she tried to tell herself it wasn't really happening now. But she couldn't stop the images and she couldn't stop the shaking.

Shouts went up from patients and physios in the dark. Antonia interpreted them as the shouts of the miners in the pit shaft. People brought torches into the physio gym, they hurried about checking that no one was hurt. To Antonia they were the lights in the miners' helmets.

She thought, I'm going to faint. . . I'm going to die here with the miner. . . An involuntary whimper trembled on her lips.

'What's the matter, Staff?' Eddy's voice of

concern was like a booming sound. He kept asking, but she couldn't answer. 'Let's get out of here,' he said, and began to wheel the chair himself.

As her only support moved away from her, Antonia gripped tightly and followed. Once in the main Reception the noise was deafening and terrifying to her. She saw the small corridor leading from the department out into the main hospital, and she gripped the chair and bolted for the light.

Hurtling headlong into the main corridor, she was unaware of everything but her own flight and so smashed the wheelchair straight into the shins of Rolf McMaster.

'For God's sake, woman,' he rasped, 'haven't we got enough patients in this hospital without you making more?' He bent to rub his leg and frowned up at her.

But when he saw her face distorted by panic he stopped and put his arm about her shoulder. 'What's the problem, Staff?'

She was still violently trembling. Now she was in the light she was beginning to make sense of the situation, but only beginning. Fractured images of fear still spun in her head.

Eddy spoke up. 'I don't know if she's OK or not. All the lights went out in the gym, and all over the department there was chaos. She might have knocked into something in the dark.'

The physiatrist—the doctor in charge of the rehabilitation unit—came running out of Physio.

'What the hell's going on in your department?' Rolf demanded. 'It looks like a black hole from here!'

'Damn right,' the physiatrist replied. 'Bloody management mess. The engineering department say they sent us a memo saying all electricity would be shut down between three and four this afternoon, but I never received any such communication.'

'Is anyone hurt in there?' Rolf indicated the department with his chin.

'No, thank goodness.' Then, looking at Antonia, who was as white as a sheet, the physiatrist added, 'I don't know about your staff nurse, though.'

Rolf asked quietly. 'Did you stumble and knocked into something?'

Antonia had to conceal the truth. She was thoroughly ashamed of panicking and being the recipient of all this concern. After all, she was a nurse, she should be calm, controlled and helping others.

'It's nothing. . .really. I think I'm coming down with a summer cold. It was a shock in there. . . I thought I was going to faint.' Rolf's arm grasped more tightly about her.

The physiatrist mumbled something about going to Engineering to give them a piece of his mind and he rushed off.

Rolf fished in his trouser pocket and produced a coin. 'Here, Eddy, be a good fellow and go and buy me a daily newspaper from that newsagent in the main hall. You shouldn't have any problem with the lift, the call buttons are all waist-high.'

After another concerned glance at Antonia, Eddy wheeled himself away. Rolf and Antonia were alone in the hallway.

He felt for her pulse. 'Toni, your heart's beating as if the very Prince of Darkness had been chasing you!'

At the mention of the word 'darkness' she shuddered and pressed up against the white coat that he was wearing. The white colour and the smell of starch seemed so reassuring to her.

Both his arms encircled her protectively. Held snugly against his broad chest like this, she felt as if she had found a safe harbour. He held her until her breathing became more normal and she had stopped shuddering.

His eyes were very calm as he asked, 'You don't feel faint now, do you?'

The inert feeling that had frozen all her voluntary movement and her common-sense thinking had almost faded. 'I'm fine now—thank you.'

'I think I'd better take you to Sick Bay right now. You still look too pale for my liking.'

'No. . .really, I'll be fine. It was just the shock.'

'I should damn well think it was,' he ground out.

Mobilising every ounce of strength she had, she disengaged herself from his arms. In reality she would have liked to have stayed there safe and protected forever.

'I must get back to the ward. Where's Eddy?' She looked about.

'We'll catch up with him.'

She felt very trembly as they walked towards the lift, and she was glad Rolf still held her arm. Just his nearness gave her strength.

In the main hall Eddy sailed up to them. 'You look a whole lot better now, Staff. You gave me a fright, looking like a ghost!'

She reassured him. All this ridiculous fuss, and all because of her fear. It was a real phobia to her now. And, what was worse, it could strike anywhere.

On the ward Sister came quickly to the rescue. 'Appalling thing to have happened!' she clucked.

'Luckily no one was seriously hurt. Now leave Staff Nurse Moore with me, Mr McMaster. I'll see to her.'

Again Antonia was led away. In the ward kitchen Sister made a strong cup of tea and ordered her to take two aspirins. 'Go to bed early tonight, Staff. And if the flu really hits you tomorrow, don't come in to work.'

'I'm sure I'll be fine.' Antonia felt embarrassed. She didn't like all this lying. But she didn't dare tell the truth, because she might put her job in jeopardy.

Once back in her flat she felt normal again—at least her body did. Her heart-rate and breathing were steady and she wasn't bathed in a cold sweat.

But she felt alone and more vulnerable than at any other time in her life. She missed Lindain dreadfully. She virtually never saw him; his studies consumed all his free time.

She convinced herself that everything would be all right once they were married. It was just this period of waiting for the exams and the consultancy post that would be trying.

Even more than before, it was vitally important that she help Lindain in every possible way. Unfortunately, that included being nice to Rolf McMaster. To Antonia, his ridiculous accusations against Lindain stemmed from the fact that he wanted her as a sex object when Kay was unavailable. By rejecting him, she was denting his sexual ego.

It was true that he had behaved most caringly and compassionately to her when she had rushed out of Physio this afternoon. But then there was that side to his nature. She had witnessed it many times when he treated his patients. She sighed. Things would be far less complicated if she could just plain hate him.

On Monday morning Rolf sat at his desk in the outpatient orthopaedic clinic. 'You look much better than when I last saw you, Toni, and thanks for coming along again to lend a hand. This sickness seems to be getting worse for my clinic sister.'

'What exactly is the matter? Is it likely to go on for a long time?'

His soft chuckle made her open her eyes wide. 'It'll be self-limiting. It's a common occupational hazard.'

Antonia's brow crinkled. Did Rolf have to talk in riddles?

'Getting pregnant is a hazard of marriage—a very normal one, though. She's got early morning sickness.'

Now Antonia understood.

Rolf stopped smiling and looked at her very

seriously. 'Love, marriage and babies, that's the prescribed order to my way of thinking. You would do well to remember that, Toni. Get the sequence wrong, and life might become far too complex.' He continued to stare hard at her as if to emphasise his point.

That was a nasty barbed remark aimed at Lindain and myself, she thought resentfully. But she decided not to rise to his needling. She would ignore all such veiled or not so veiled accusations. She hoped this morning's clinic wasn't going to be too difficult.

No further problems arose until Antonia was helping Mrs Horton to dress. Rolf had examined her feet and diagnosed a treatment without surgical intervention. Mrs Horton was in her late sixties and she was a huge woman, carrying far too much weight. But she was jolly, and she had been very pleased with Rolf's fastidious examination and explanation of treatment.

'Ouch!' Mrs Horton's face crinkled with pain as she tried to push her arm through the sleeve of her raincoat.

'Your shoulder's very painful,' Antonia observed. 'There was nothing about it in the letter from your GP.'

'No, dear,' Mrs Horton shook her head as if to shake off the pain, 'it's nothing really. And it is easing. I didn't like to trouble my GP, he's so busy.'

'But you could have mentioned it to Mr McMaster this morning. He's the specialist in conditions like this. Stay here, Mrs Horton,' advised Antonia. 'I'm sure Mr McMaster won't mind taking a look.'

Rolf was viewing an X-ray when Antonia said, 'Excuse me, sir, but I think you've missed something on Mrs Horton.'

He raised one sardonic black eyebrow. 'A few nights of individual study with Smythe and you think you know more than a consultant now.'

'I didn't mean that, sir.' Inwardly she grimaced at her poor choice of words. 'Mrs Horton has shoulder pain. I noticed when I was helping her put on her coat.'

His face softened. 'Why don't patients tell their doctors? Surely I'm not so unapproachable?'

'She doesn't want to be a bother. She thinks everyone is too busy.'

In the examination cubicle once more Rolf began, 'Now, let's have a look at this shoulder.'

Antonia helped undress the patient, and then assisted her to get back on to the plinth.

'Now tell me, how did the pain come on? I can see you have difficulty taking off your dress, and I know Staff Nurse is very considerate.'

'Oh, this is embarrassing.' Mrs Horton was covered in confusion. 'You see, the way it happened—well. . .it was a bit saucy.'

Rolf's voice hardly hid his amusement. 'Come, come, Mrs Horton, now you've thoroughly intrigued Staff Nurse and myself, you can't keep the story to yourself!'

There was a moment's silence before the patient plucked up courage. 'I was taking Bonzo for an early walk—he's our boxer dog—and he saw. . .a lady dog on the other side of the road. Well, he took off after her, and really jerked my shoulder.'

'Aha. . .' Rolf coughed discreetly behind his hand. 'So the dog almost dislocated your shoulder, eh? It would be better for your musculo-skeletal system if Bonzo led a more celibate life.'

'Oh, no, sir, you can't put all the blame on our Bonzo. He's a champion and a stud dog.'

Antonia thought she was going to burst into laughter, Mrs Horton was defending Bonzo so assiduously.

The patient continued. 'It was that little bitch of a Pekinese. She had her tail and head up, and the way she waggled her little behind. . .well she could have taught a night-walker a thing or two!'

Rolf laughed outright. 'Undue provocation, I

see! All right, Bonzo gets a reprieve from me. Now tell me, when did the pain come on?'

'Straight away, then it wasn't so bad for a few days. An ache started around the shoulder.' Mrs Horton rubbed the whole area. 'And then it seemed to go down to the elbow.'

'How long ago was this?'

'A couple of months. As I said to Nurse here, it's easing now.'

'Can you lie on that shoulder at night?' he asked.

'No, I have to stay off it.'

Rolf continued his in-depth questioning. 'Is the shoulder painful even when you keep your arm still and by your side?'

'No.'

He then went through a thorough examination of her neck.

'Why do you look at my neck?' she asked.

'Because some shoulder pain can arise from the joints there. I don't think you have any problem in your neck, though.'

His examination of her shoulder was equally fastidious. When he had finished he stood back and indicated Antonia to help dress the patient.

'You have what we call a frozen shoulder, Mrs Horton. It's a painful restricting injury, as you well know. I'm sending you to X-Ray for neck and shoulder pictures, but that's just precautionary. I don't think we'll find anything sinister. Your main treatment, then, will be in Physio.'

'What'll they do there?' she wanted to know.

'The capsule of your shoulder joint is very tight. They'll ice the area, then use gentle stretching techniques to loosen up the tight fibres surrounding the joint. That'll free it up and you'll be able to move.'

'Well, I'm glad Nurse here found me out, so to speak.'

'I have a good team,' he assured Mrs Horton.

At the end of Clinic, when Antonia was changing the linen on the examination couches, Rolf came in and said, 'Are you wearing fancy dress at the Summer Ball on Friday?'

She was taken aback by his personal question. 'No, just a long evening dress.'

'That surprises me, Toni. I thought you'd enjoy dressing up for a bit of fun.'

She turned away from his direct gaze and busied herself smoothing out a sheet. Why did he continue to stand there? She felt forced to say something more.

'What are you going to dress up in?' She felt like asking if he was going as Bluebeard, but she thought of Lindain and didn't say anything.

'Nothing out of character.'

She wondered what that meant.

'That reminds me, I must pick up my evening suit from the cleaners.'

A wicked glint lit his eyes. What was behind that conspiratorial look? she wondered. It was a good job Lindain would be with her that night. She felt there was something secretive behind Rolf's smile.

CHAPTER SEVEN

'I'm so upset, Toni. Clients can be really trying at times. The one I went to see today changes her mind more frequently than her underwear. I wouldn't mind, but she hasn't commissioned several sets of French knickers.'

Antonia sat on the chesterfield in her flat and stared at her brother. Rupert's face was taut. She thought he'd burst into tears at any moment. And she felt very distressed for him.

'What's wrong with this beautiful ballgown? It looks absolutely out of this world to me.' She took the dress from Rupert and started to remove the protective plastic wrapping.

'The colour! She's decided that she doesn't want ivory. She wants it in midnight-blue.'

Antonia ran her fingers over the silk taffeta. 'So you've got to make the whole thing up again, before you can present the bill.'

'Yes. It's the money that matters at the moment. Clients forget that we have to buy the materials first, and Rosalind and I have no capital to fall back on.'

Antonia would have lent her brother the

money, but she knew he had a fierce pride. 'It's a pity Dad's will is so watertight. You'll be worth quite a bit of money in ten years' time.'

'So will you.'

Antonia had an idea, and one, she thought, that would help both herself and Rupert.

'What size is this dress?' she asked.

'A twelve.'

'Would it fit me? It looks and feels gorgeous. I'd love to be able to wear it at the Summer Ball tonight. I'd pay you for it, of course.'

Rupert's face lit up. 'It might just fit you, Toni. I could do a lightning refit if it doesn't.'

In the bedroom, in front of the long mirror of her wardrobe, Antonia felt a flutter of excitement as Rupert helped her into the dress. It was styled along Regency lines, with a very full skirt and a slight train at the back. And it had an eggshell-blue wide sash that would fit under the bustline. This would be tied at the back in a big bow, the tails of which would almost reach the floor.

Antonia felt herself breathing in hard as Rupert pulled the bodice around her. 'Oh, it's far too tight!' She was very disappointed.

'No, no problem, Toni. Luckily I made it up with room to spare in the darts. I can let them out in minutes.'

What Antonia couldn't see was Rupert deliberately pulling the dress tight at the back, and smirking to himself.

Antonia was delighted with the dress when Rupert had finished the alterations. He had sat with his back to her, tailor-fashion, in front of her window for the light. And she hadn't actually seen him unpick any stitches because he had demanded that she fetch him a Coke from the store next door.

'And I've got two other items to set your appearance off tonight.' Rupert reached into a box and produced a reticule that exactly matched the dress and a small black velvet bandit mask.

He placed the mask over her face.

'I don't know that I'm too keen on it.' She was doubtful.

'It's a must,' Rupert encouraged. 'It'll add the final touch to a night of intrigue.'

She was convinced. And the outfit was perfect. Lindain would approve, because it wasn't too childish, yet it made Antonia feel as if she was in costume.

Rupert would only take a cheque for the cost of the materials, he wouldn't charge for labour, even though Antonia tried to insist.

Lindain loved the dress, and to Antonia's surprise he loved the mask too. He even thought it a pity that Rupert hadn't been around to make one for him.

She felt very happy as she walked into the ballroom. She thought Lindain looked so handsome in his formal black evening suit.

It was a perfect warm night. Even at ten o'clock, as the night began to blacken, it was still comfortable enough to walk outside. Antonia was glad she was with Lindain because the night sky was cloudy and when the moon was obscured it was too dark for her liking.

But her happiness was cut short when Lindain's chief called him away. Antonia's fears were realised as Lindain walked back dejectedly.

'I'm sorry, Antonia, I've been called in, and there's no arguing about it. I've already tried. There's some emergency at the Royal and the stand-by anaesthetist is in theatre with another patient.'

Lindain had been so charming all evening, just as he had been after her parents had died. Antonia, although bitterly disappointed, tried not to let it show, especially as he would have to concentrate in theatre.

'I'll have to take the car, but here's Charlie. He'll look after you and take you home. He's a houseman from the psychiatric unit.'

Antonia shook hands and was introduced to a young man in a gorilla suit. He pulled her on to the dance-floor and began to gyrate in front of her.

'I've got these gorilla movements down pat,' he explained from behind his rubbery mask. 'I even went to the zoo to study them!'

Although she felt piqued at Lindain's leaving, and the thought of dancing cheek to cheek with one of nature's big apes hadn't been her idea of a night out, Antonia made an effort to look pleased.

The fast music stopped and the band struck up a slow number.

'My dance, I believe.'

A very tall man strode up between Charlie and Antonia. He was dressed in a formal black tail suit with satin-faced lapels. His white bow-tie was elegantly tied beneath the wing collar of his sparkling white shirt.

But it was his head and his hand that completely stunned Antonia. He wore the most magnificent hawk's head and his white gloves were covered in blue-grey feathers.

She stared up into the wine-red eyes that glittered out of a feathered face. Beneath his eyes the colour was yellow and black and his throat was the shade of an orangy conker.

'Hey, butt out, buddy!' Charlie the gorilla was asserting himself. 'I'm looking after this young lady.'

The hawk's voice was full of controlled power. He spoke slowly. 'The young lady wants to glide and soar when she dances. She doesn't want to gyrate like a creature suddenly attacked by a horde of stinging ants.'

The hawkman swung around and Charlie was ushered into a corner. Antonia couldn't see or hear exactly what went on, but the upshot was that Charlie scuttled away and the hawk was by her side again.

'Would you care to dance inside or out on the terrace?'

'You may be dressed as a magnificent bird of prey, but you have the manners of a common boar!' she snapped furiously.

'The buffet here is more than adequate, your gorilla will be perfectly happy once he finds a banana.'

She felt she was being guided out on to the terrace which now was floodlit by a full moon.

'Don't think you can put your talons on me,' said Antonia, as she jerked her arm out of his grasp.

'You have nothing to fear. They'll always be hooded when I'm with you.'

A *frisson* of fear shuddered down her spine. She felt his arms slide about her as he took up his position to dance.

She struggled to free herself. The train of her dress was awkward, she stepped back on to it and almost fell. The hawkman held her fast against his body.

Swiftly she bent to pick up the train and throw it to one side so that she could make her escape.

Her eyes were shining and angry. 'I won't dance with you. Even if I wanted to, this dress is impossible.'

'Your dress is wonderful. You look beautiful in it.'

She stared hard into those red, unseeing eyes. They were made of glass. The more she stared the more compelling she found his looks. It was as if he held her by some mesmeric spell.

He spoke slowly. 'There should be a time for dressing up and having fun. Hospital work can be depressing, even unbearably tragic at times.'

Who was this man behind the mask of feathers? Suddenly she wanted to know.

'My compliments to your tailor. He's done a marvellous job of concealing your tail feathers in that evening suit with tails,' she told him.

His laugh was deep-throated and somewhat familiar. 'Tonight could be fun if you ruffled my feathers a little.'

She felt completely out of her depth. The conversation had taken on a tone of sensuality that she didn't like. Why hadn't she just walked off and left this stranger?

'Don't you know me, Toni?'

She stood transfixed as the man removed his mask.

Familiar grey eyes dancing with humorous lights assailed hers, beneath the black hair that had tumbled down on to his forehead.

'Rolf!'

'You're right—your brother has done an exquisite job on the head and the hands of my costume. And my tailor in Savile Row will be pleased to hear you approve of his evening suit.'

Antonia was momentarily stunned. 'I might have known my brother was behind this somehow!' She eyed Rolf with a sullen scrutiny. 'I only hope Rupert charged you an arm and a leg for that get-up.'

'A wing and a claw at least. But it's been worth every penny just to see your reaction.'

She brushed rudely past him and made her way into the throng of people on the dance-floor. Scanning the scene, she looked desperately for Charlie the gorilla. He was nowhere in sight. Rolf had put the frighteners on him all right!

Antonia didn't have to look round, she could feel Rolf's presence behind her. Kicking out her skirt, she made her way defiantly into the hall of the hotel. If she couldn't find Charlie she'd phone for a taxi.

Everything seemed to stack up against her. There was no one on the reception desk, and to her annoyance she found she had no money in her reticule, only a front door key.

Angrily she tore off the bandit mask that her brother had given her. A night of intrigue, he had promised her. But she would foil his plot. She was going to have nothing more to do with Rolf.

'I can see this evening has become very tedious for you, Toni, so I'll take you home.'

Rolf's cool assumption vexed her beyond belief. 'I won't accept your kind offer.' She glared up at him. 'I'll walk home if necessary.' And she made for the entrance and out on to the hotel front.

Soft laughter close to her ear nearly drove her temper sky-high. 'Your dress certainly wasn't made for hiking, Toni. And the night is pitch-black out there. You forget we're in the middle of the countryside.'

She had momentarily forgotten. Oh, why hadn't this ball been held in the centre of town?

'Charlie must be around here somewhere.' She spoke to herself, her words barely audible. Her desire to get away from Rolf was intense.

'The last time I saw a gorilla he was heading west—no doubt on his way to the Empire State Building to bat a few aeroplanes out of the sky.'

She looked sharply into his amused, stubborn

eyes. 'You may think you're funny, but I certainly don't!' she snapped.

His tone was low now. 'Your Dr Lindain Smythe wouldn't like to have you walk home alone at night. So why not accept my offer to take you safely there? After all, I'm Smythe's superior, and he has to follow my orders.'

Antonia felt trapped. She was afraid of the night outside. Rolf seemed the lesser evil.

'Thank you,' she said stiffly, and was promptly guided to his Range Rover. He helped her up the high steps.

'I'm sorry the transport isn't as elegant as I'd have liked for tonight. But my blackbird family are still in residence.'

She hardly had time to take in his words before he climbed in beside her.

'Hold my hand,' he ordered.

She glanced at him coldly.

'Both my hands.'

His feathered gloves tumbled on to her skirt.

'And I would appreciate it if you'd let me rest my head on your lap.'

The hawk head was placed firmly in front of her. The soft smooth feathers felt velvety against her hands.

'You're playing with words,' she muttered defiantly. 'I don't like your games.'

He took no notice. She was aware that he

concentrated hard on the road in the dim light of his headlights up front.

She was sure he would ask to come into her flat for a coffee. She would feign a headache. But this ploy was thwarted. Rolf's pager bleeped just as they were pulling up outside her door.

'May I use your phone?' he asked. 'It's probably the hospital.' She couldn't refuse. Once inside her door he ran ahead up the stairs. 'Where's your phone?'

'In the bedroom.' Unfortunately, she thought.

Antonia paced her sitting-room until she thought she heard him ring off. Then she stood still. She was listening for him to come out of her bedroom. There was no way she would go to him.

Suddenly he was with her, and he looked concerned.

'Was there a problem with anyone at the Royal?' she queried.

'No, it was about another patient at another hospital.'

'You'll have to go straight there now.' She tried not to sound too pleased.

'They're doing fine. I'd asked for a progress report, that's all.' Rolf undid his white tie and loosened his stiff collar. His eyes penetrated hers with a frankness that made her blush. When he took her hand in his she froze.

'I see Smythe hasn't made an honest woman of you yet.' He looked pointedly at her bare ring finger. 'Has he made a dishonest woman of you, I wonder?'

Swiftly she raised her right hand to slap him hard across his insolent face, but he caught her by the wrist and stayed her blow.

'If you defend your virginity as passionately as that, then you're a very desirable lady indeed, Toni.'

His arms were about her holding her fast. His lips came down on her cheek close to her mouth as she averted her face.

'You're the biggest bastard I've ever known——'

Her words were silenced as his mouth found hers. The fragrance of his aftershave, the warm insistence as his tongue probed her mouth, all wrought their artful spell. She tried to push against his broad chest, but his will was stronger. His sensuality crept up and flowed over her, weakening her resistance, spreading waves of unwanted sensual delight through her body.

She despised her body for its physical treachery. But she found her response of anger turning to want.

A moment of sanity flashed across her mind as she felt Rolf tug at the big blue bow at her back. The material loosened and fell to the floor.

Over his shoulder she saw the flat-warming present Rupert had given her. It was the picture of the hawk in evening dress with the lady in Regency costume.

She pushed Rolf away and spat out, 'That wretch Rupert! I see you and he have connived to have me dressed like this. And I paid for the costume——'

'No.' Rolf produced a piece of paper from his breast pocket. 'Here's your cheque.' He held it up for her to see, then tossed it aside.

'I suppose you think you have the right to undress me if you've paid for this gown!' She was furious!

'I would like the right to undress you any time,' he muttered thickly, and Antonia kicked out at his shins.

He caught her again in his arms. 'Why do you freeze your heart against me, Toni? You know we're made for each other. Why resist when we could find such ecstasy together?'

No one had ever spoken so openly or directly to her before in her life. Suddenly the fight had gone out of her. She shuddered as the dress fell away from her body, and Rolf picked her up and carried her into the bedroom.

On the bed he covered her and kissed her passionately. Every fibre of her body tingled alive. His masculine touch melted her reserve, the heat of his body inflamed her too, and drove an exciting, pulsing desire through her.

She wanted him close, and closer still——

The telephone shrilled in her ear. It was like an alarm bringing reality back to her sensually drugged mind.

'Leave it.' Rolf's command came close to her cheek.

It must be Lindain, she thought, and reached out.

Rolf's fingers dug painfully into her rib-cage, but she had to speak. She knew it was Lindain. 'Hello. . .'

'Sorry, darling, I'm still back here in the hospital. It's been one hell of a night in Casualty. I won't be through until early morning.'

'Oh, no!'

'Can't talk any longer, Antonia—I'm needed. Love you. Bye.'

Rolf's voice was urgent. 'Tell him you're through with him. . . Tell him now.' His leg thrust between hers, and he held her tighter, so that she could say nothing. Rolf grabbed the phone, but it went dead.

'Why didn't you kick him out of your life once and for all?'

Antonia struggled and wriggled herself free from his weight, for reality was painfully dawning.

Shoes and clothes were scattered on the floor,

and quickly she bent to pick them up. Then, facing him, she flung the clothes at him. 'You've conned your way here by disguise and deceit. Now get out!'

His narrowed eyes burned brightly. 'You're the one who's being deceived, Toni. I bet right now Smythe is enjoying some very intimate therapy with a certain voluptuous staff nurse from theatre.'

'You're disgusting and hateful!' Her emotions seethed as she looked at him. Seeing him lying on her rumpled bed with his hair in disarray, she was reminded that it would only have taken her a few minutes more to have been completely unfaithful to Lindain.

'Just go!' she blurted out.

Then her most fearful nightmare returned. The bedroom light, the street lights, the neon advertising on the pub, all went out. The darkness was sudden and suffocating.

Old fears and primal panic beat up inside her. She must have light. She must dispel the darkness.

Her armoury of weapons against the blackness was in the drawer of her bedside table. She jerked the handle violently and the drawer slid out and her torch, candle and matches all spilled on to the floor.

Desperately she scrabbled about trying to find

them, but they all eluded her. She knocked up against something. It was Rolf.

Almost hysterically she clung to him. Remembering the time she had run out of Physio, she sought shelter and comfort against his body. But no strong arms encircled her this time. No protective voice soothed her.

'Don't go!' she cried. 'Don't. . . Stay with me tonight.' She sounded pathetic.

As unexpectedly as the lights had failed, they suddenly came on again.

She felt herself being flung on the bed, and heard Rolf's voice, full of pain.

'You can't turn a man on and off like a light switch.' In the full blaze of her bedroom she saw him hastily dressing. 'There are some very Anglo-Saxon words to describe the sort of tease you are, Toni!'

She was mortified. Her body still trembled, but it shuddered even more violently as he strode away and slammed her front door.

It had been an appalling night. She never wanted to recall a single moment of it again. She never wanted to face Rolf. . .ever.

CHAPTER EIGHT

'I WANT to talk to you, Toni.'

Antonia was early for work the following morning and had parked her car in the staff car park. Nothing had prepared her for this unforeseen encounter with Rolf.

She was filled with a rising tide of guilt and shame. Guilt because she had almost totally deceived Lindain, and shame because of her panic attack of last night. Turning away from him, she locked her car door. But she had parked close to the wall and close to the next car. Now Rolf barred her escape.

'I've been thinking about you,' he said. 'And I know you've got a phobia about the dark.'

This stunned her. She turned her head away. 'I don't know what you're talking about.'

'You panicked when the lights went out in Physio. You had another panic attack last night when we were in your bedroom.'

With a supreme effort to sound controlled she said, 'You're completely wrong. Now, let me pass and go in to work.'

'It's nothing to be ashamed of. You need help.

Obviously something very traumatic has happened to you. Fear of the dark is a common, classic phobia. In your case it's developed into a full-blown syndrome that's invading your life.'

Hearing her inner self revealed so clearly, she immediately put up defensive walls. 'I don't know what you think you're playing at now. Surely dressing up as a hawk was enough fantasy for you?'

'Don't be stupid!' Rolf gripped her shoulder. 'You can't hide this from me, Toni. I know you too well.' He took a deep breath and continued more gently. 'Fear is a natural body reaction. If you lived in prehistoric times and you bumped into a dinosaur, you'd be foolish if you didn't run away.'

'So now you're talking of dinosaurs! If you want to play fantasy games where you're a caveman then count me out. I've no intention of being pulled about by my long hair!' Inside she was trembling. It took all her control not to show her real feelings.

'Don't be silly!' His tone was full of irritation. 'Nature has provided us with a wonderful nervous system. It functions beautifully under ordinary circumstances. But—and you know this, Toni—it functions against you in a phobic situation.'

She looked at the ground. She felt he would never stop relentlessly pushing home his points.

'Hippocrates wrote about a man who was afraid of nightfall. And Augustus Caesar couldn't sit in the dark. Nowadays phobias are recognised for what they are, and there are some excellent desensitisation programmes. Let me help you. . . I can refer you to someone who can put this problem out of your life.'

'I have no such problem,' she denied vehemently, and looked him in the eye. 'If I have any I'll consult Dr Lindain Smythe.'

'Smythe!' he sneered. 'Don't try and tell me you've got this wonderful relationship, because I don't believe it. He doesn't know anything about your phobia——'

Antonia couldn't bear any more. She brushed past him and ran into the hospital. Everything Rolf said was true—she knew it. But she pushed it out of her mind. The Physio incident and the one in her bedroom were chances in a million. It would never happen to her again.

Antonia was taking TPRs on the main ward when she saw Eddy in the sun-room. He had got himself out of bed and was now leaning on the narrow window-sill, looking wistfully outside. His crutches lay discarded untidily on the floor.

After writing up a patient's recordings she

walked quietly up behind him. Micahel was engrossed in one of his sci-fi books, so he didn't see her. She tapped Eddy lightly on the shoulder. The surprise startled him and he had to grab hold of the sill to stay upright.

'You should have a nurse with you, even for short walks,' she admonished.

'He was doing fine until you nearly frightened him out of his skin,' said Michael behind her.

Antonia guided Eddy to a chair. 'You're no help, Michael, and you promised to keep an eye on Eddy.'

'He *was* keeping an eye on me, Staff,' Eddy defended his mate.

'I've had this out with you so many times. Really, you two are no help to each other.'

'Oh, stop fussing!' Michael was testy. 'Nothing would have happened if you hadn't crept up like that.'

'Your mind is permanently in outer space, Michael. Your sci-fi books rocket you out of the real world.'

'That's why I read them. I'm bored to death lying here all the time.'

She knew Michael's progress was tantalisingly slow for him. 'I can see you're getting depressed,' she agreed. 'But didn't Mr McMaster say you'd be on the tilt table at the end of next week if your back continued to improve?'

Michael ran his hands through his hair. 'That's something. . . I know. OK, I'll keep an eagle eye on Eddy for you. He's restless today because there's no workout in the Physio gym on Saturdays.'

Antonia laid her hand on Eddy's shoulder. 'I hear you were doing stairs in the gym on Friday.'

Eddy looked downcast. 'Only tiddly ones—six up and six down.'

'How many do you have to do at home?'

'A hundred and ninety-two—I live in a top flat.'

'Heavens!' Antonia covered her eyes. 'The physio will have to take you up and down some main hospital stairs before you're discharged.'

'That's what I keep asking to do,' he told her sullenly. 'But they say I'm not ready.'

'It's best to take things literally one step at a time. You and Michael are in the doldrums right now, but things'll pick up, you'll see.'

She took their TPRs, then said, 'I know you teach, Michael, but what age-group?'

'Adults,' he replied.

'So you work at a college, then?'

'Yes—university.'

'And do you teach science there?' She picked up his fiction book.

'Well, I'm a researcher in nuclear physics. But I do a little lecturing.'

'He's Professor Michael,' Eddy announced behind her.

Antonia laughed. She had imagined Michael taught teenage boys. 'You don't look like a boffin to me, Michael. And how do these crazy fiction stories help in your work?'

'Today's fantasy is tomorrow's science,' he said seriously. 'Don't forget H. G. Wells and Jules Verne. Sometimes people say or write crazy things, but in time they're proved to be absolutely right.'

Antonia thought of Rolf. He was right about her phobia. It was crazy not to seek help. But she couldn't face up to it.

'Here, Staff, have a chocolate.' Michael indicated a box on top of his locker.

When she opened the lid Antonia gave him a jaundiced stare. 'I'd love one, only they're all gone.' Then she laughed.

Eddy and Michael grinned. Michael said, 'Sorry, I didn't realise my visitors had scoffed the lot. Here, let me have the lid.' She handed it to him, and he tore off a red bow that decorated one corner. 'Here's a present from Eddy and myself. Neither of us means to play you up.'

The bow was flat and large with free ends a couple of inches long. Antonia thanked them both. It was a fun present, with no real value.

But it was the sort of thing that made all the hard work of nursing worthwhile.

Later that morning Antonia was lifting a full bag of soiled linen into the laundry chute when Sister Cook came up.

'Here, let me help you with that, Staff. It's always a better lifting technique with two, and I don't want you off duty with a bad back. Not now I've just got you.' She smiled warmly.

'Thanks, Sister.' The two of them managed the bulky item quite easily.

To her surprise Antonia found Sister following her into the linen cupboard. As she fixed a new bag on to the skip the older woman's tone was friendly.

'How are you settling in, Staff?'

'Fine, thank you,' Antonia replied. 'I love orthopaedics.'

'That's evident. I can see you get on well with the patients, especially Eddy.'

'He's easy to like, and he's so good and brave.' Antonia spoke quietly. 'Even if I have to scold him occasionally for trying to be too independent too early.'

Sister nodded. There was a moment's silence. 'I hear the Summer Ball was very entertaining last night. Did you enjoy yourself?'

Immediately Antonia was on the defensive. Had Sister heard on the grapevine that she had gone to the ball with Lindain but left with Rolf? 'It was a brilliant evening,' she replied, choosing her words carefully. 'The food and the band were excellent.' She avoided Sister's eyes.

'Hospitals are romantic places.' Sister sounded concerned. 'It's natural for passions to flare and die quickly. . .'

Antonia started to blush. She thought Sister had somehow heard that Rolf had stayed at her flat. She said nothing, but fumbled with the skip.

'Now if you have any problems—any problems at all—while you're here at the Royal, Antonia, don't hesitate to come to me.'

Blushing a deeper red, Antonia said, 'Thanks, I'll remember.' She was sure Sister had found her out, and that she thought she was two-timing Lindain.

In fact, the very opposite was the truth. Sister knew Lindain to be multiple-timing her staff nurse. But she let the matter lie, thinking it best not to probe deeper.

Wriggling her toes in her duty shoes, Antonia reflected on the morning. Her feet ached. She'd been running around like something demented, and so had the rest of the staff on ward eight.

Now she pushed her empty fruit salad bowl away. She had taken a very late lunch and only a few other people remained in the staff canteen.

It was going to be even harder work on the ward from now on. Several new admissions had been accommodated that morning. They were all fractured femurs that needed to be slung in traction. There were patients in the middle of the ward, some even in the little corridor leading to the kitchen and the dressings-room.

Sister had almost flung up her arms in despair. She'd hoped there weren't going to be any more admissions. And when one came she'd put him in the sitting-room. If anyone else was admitted he'd have to go in the main corridor, and Sister wasn't having that.

Antonia's mind was a fog when she thought of all the work.

'What the hell have you been up to with McMaster?' Lindain's voice was unnaturally high.

'Me?' Antonia jerked round as Lindain pulled a chair up close beside her. She thought for sure that her time with Rolf was now common knowledge.

'Yes, you!' She'd never seen him look so peeved. 'God, that man's got a dirty laugh! And to think you're the cause of it!'

She felt herself prickling with a sudden flush of heat. Rolf couldn't have said anything about last night, could he?

'It was terribly embarrassing in theatre this

morning,' Lindain lowered his voice. 'Just as McMaster was sewing up the last patient, he started to laugh. Of course, everyone wanted to know what was so funny, but he wouldn't say.'

Antonia went cold. She had no idea what was coming.

'Then later, in front of the rest of the surgical team, he clapped me on the back and told me to ask you—and I quote—"the one about the fat lady's bum".'

Antonia was astonished.

'Have you been telling McMaster blue jokes?' Lindain went on. 'If so, I think it's very unbecoming.'

'Lindain, how can you believe anything like that about me? You know I can't tell jokes. I never remember the punch lines.'

'Well, whatever you told McMaster, it carried some sort of punch. And fancy using the word "bum" to a consultant. Couldn't you have used "bottom" or "behind"? The way he laughed,' Lindain covered his face, 'anyone would think you'd delivered a rugby joke!'

Now Antonia was peeved. 'Look here, Lindain, if I had repeated a rugby joke, and I haven't, then the chosen word wouldn't have been "bum". It would have been something far more asinine!'

'Oh, really, Antonia——'

'I never imagined you to be such a prude, Lindain. Anyway, I haven't told McMaster a joke. That phrase was just something one of my patients dreamed up for himself. And he used it when I was helping McMaster change a dressing.'

She couldn't imagine why Rolf had chosen that moment in time to allude to the incident. And he had done it in the most convoluted and calculated way. She concluded that he was trying to stir up trouble between Lindain and herself. And he'd succeeded!

Lindain continued to look aggrieved. 'Whatever really happened, the incident has caused me a great deal of embarrassment. I've been getting some very funny looks from the theatre staff. A future consultant should have an exemplary background. If underlings are to carry out my orders, then they should look up to me.'

Antonia was seeing a side of Lindain that frankly she despised.

'As a future consultant's wife you should be an asset, Antonia, not a liability,' he went on.

That did it! Antonia delivered her words with force. 'I believe the sequence is engagement, then marriage, Lindain, and I'm not engaged. And the next man I go out with will be a teacher or an architect. At least they're not called out through the night. At least I'll see my husband in the evenings!'

She thrust her chair back, stood up tall, and walked briskly away. That should have some effect, she thought angrily. There were too many doctors in her life. And it all added up to double trouble.

Back on the ward she tried to appear outwardly calm, but inwardly she seethed. Rolf's tricky antics had caused a rift between Lindain and herself. Obviously that had been the consultant's intention. And both Lindain and herself had fallen right into the trap.

As she delivered bedpans for the patients and pulled the curtains around their beds, she knew she had to keep cool. If she wanted to get the better of Rolf she needed every brain cell functioning. He was so tricky. But she determined to turn the tables on him.

Rolf walked on to the ward later that afternoon. He had come to check the alignment of the tractions on his newly admitted patients. Sister was off duty, so Antonia was in charge.

As they worked together on the patients there was a professional truce between them. But when Rolf sat opposite her at Sister's desk and wrote up his notes in the patient files, she began to plot.

'Would you like a cup of tea?' she asked sweetly.

He looked up, his expression blank for a moment. 'Yes, I'd love one. Do you want to talk about something in particular, Toni?'

Ah, she laughed to herself, he thinks I'm going to ask for his help. He thinks it's about the phobia.

'No, nothing special.'

In the ward kitchen she busied herself arranging the table. She felt the red ribbon in her uniform pocket, the ribbon that had been a present from Michael and Eddy. Yes, it would do very well for her purpose.

Rolf sat back nonchalantly in his chair, his long legs stretched beneath the table. He was absorbed in his pocket diary.

He looks very much at home, she thought as she poured milk into a jug. Just as if we were a married couple. She banished the thought immediately. The idea was intolerable.

'Do you take sugar?'

'Yes, thank you.' He was being very careful and polite to her.

Concealing her actions from his view, she reached into the drawer of the kitchen table. The large wooden spoon was there, and deftly she tied the ribbon round the handle. Then she produced the sugar bowl and laid the spoon by it.

'I know there are hospital shortages, but isn't this going a bit too far?' He picked up the wooden spoon. It looked ridiculous next to the china crockery. 'I suppose we'll be using discarded surgical forceps for sugar tongs next!'

She struggled inwardly to remain calm as she said, 'I thought the wooden spoon suited your nature better. A teaspoon would have been far too small.' Her excitement was mounting. 'You're a stirrer, Rolf, and don't think you can get away with it. This morning you deliberately tried to cause friction between Lindain and myself. Well——' she was racing now '—your tactics haven't worked. And nothing you can ever dream up will cause a rift between us!'

She would never give him the satisfaction of letting him know that was exactly what had happened.

He didn't bat an eyelid. He sat there admiring the spoon. She felt very wary. She wasn't getting the reaction she expected. She was prepared for a row.

'This must be Leap Year, and this is your way of proposing, Toni.' He looked into her astonished eyes. 'It's a charming Cotswold custom. . .giving your lover a wooden spoon to symbolise your love.'

She was dumbfounded.

'But only one bowl on the spoon, my love?'

'What are you wittering on about?' She felt she would explode with rage.

'You obviously don't know, Toni. The bowls on the spoon symbolise the number of children we're going to have. And I'm quite sure we'll have more than one.'

He's raving mad, she thought, and suddenly felt weak. 'That spoon has nothing to do with love or marriage——'

'I shall treasure it always.'

She watched incredulously as he pocketed the spoon.

'Give it back, for heaven's sake! It belongs to the ward.' She felt exasperated.

'Very well, sweetheart, I understand your emotions were at work and you gave it to me on impulse. But——' Rolf removed the ribbon '—I shall keep the red ribbon, and I'll prize it always.'

Antonia was so mad she almost snatched the spoon from his hands. 'God, your conceit is unbelievable!'

A junior nurse knocked on the kitchen door. 'Excuse me, Mr McMaster, but Casualty have rung through. Would you help them with a difficult diagnosis?' She had obviously heard some part of their altercation, and now stood hovering in the doorway.

'Thank you, Nurse, I'll come at once.' Turning back to Antonia, he said softly, 'I'll take a raincheck on that cup of tea.'

She was left alone with the tea things and a boiling rage. How could that man be so cool? Did nothing ruffle him? Her pulses were racing so much she felt all her blood must be in turbulence.

Rolf had won twice that day. Certainly he had caused a rift between Lindain and herself. She would have to do something to patch that up. And he had turned her joke upside-down and made it work against her in the most unacceptable way.

Sighing to herself, she had to admit that he aroused strong emotions within her heart. But they were not connected with love.

Antonia had a couple of rest days off from work. And when she returned to the ward she was in charge, and her first problem was a mighty one.

Charge Nurse from Casualty wanted her to take another patient. His voice sounded tired. 'This young fellow's got to be admitted on to your ward, Staff. He's a paraplegic. He'll need the most stringent orthopaedic nursing care.'

Antonia groaned inwardly at the thought of

what lay ahead for this patient. 'We're absolutely chock-a-block. Let me think a second———'

'Haven't you got any ambulatory patients that could be transferred to another ward? It'll only be for a couple of days. Stoke Mandeville will take him when he's stable.'

Antonia covered her eyes. 'Yes, I've got an amp who I could transfer.' She didn't want to let Eddy go.

'Great! I know ward four have a bed vacancy.'

'I'll phone them right away and arrange things.'

The charge nurse sounded very relieved. 'You'll have a couple of hours' grace—this fellow will be in theatre for some time. But thanks for being so helpful.'

'Is the patient one of Mr McMaster's?' She hoped he was—if so, it wouldn't be difficult explaining Eddy's transfer to Rolf.

'Afraid not. He'll be under Mr Wiggins.'

'Of course.' Now Antonia remembered Rolf was operating at another orthopaedic hospital today.

'Thanks for all your help.' The charge nurse rang off.

Antonia exhaled deeply, then punched in the numbers to call the ward. It was a mixed surgical one.

'Sister Bennet speaking, ward four.'

After explaining the situation, Antonia was pleased to hear that Eddy would be welcome.

'Oh, yes, the whole hospital must know your patient.' Sister remembered all the details. 'He's a bit of a hero, isn't he?'

Antonia felt especially responsible. 'He's a good patient really. But he's over-eager. He feels his progress is too slow. Physio haven't given the all-clear for him to walk alone yet, so he must always be with a nurse.'

'Hmm. . .'

Antonia could tell Sister was taking notes. She continued, 'He tries hard to do his stump bandaging, but sometimes he gets in a bit of a mess. And. . .' Antonia didn't like spelling treatment out to another nurse, especially as she was talking to a sister. 'You do know that Mr McMaster doesn't like the word "stump" being used to his patient's face?'

Sister's voice held a smile. 'Don't worry, Staff. I may be a surgical sister, but I married an amp and my husband works as a prosthetist-orthotist here at the Limb-Fitting Centre. And I'll look after Eddy myself.'

'Things couldn't have worked out better!' Antonia was delighted. She needn't worry about Eddy. In fact, if he knew that Sister had married an amp he might ask her questions that he wouldn't put to another nurse.

'Just one more thing. . . His temperature has always been up, just a little. We can't work it out, but there's been no purulent discharge from his wound.'

'OK, I've noted it all down. He'll be very welcome here.' They said their goodbyes.

The rest of the ward staff needed to be informed of the change, so Antonia called an informal meeting. Her nurses all looked exhausted as it was.

'I'll do my best to get extra help,' she told them, 'but in the meantime it'll be heavy going. However, the new patient will only be with us for a few days, then he'll go to Stoke Mandeville.'

An older nursing auxiliary spoke up. 'It's the best place for spinal injuries. They have the facilities, the expertise and all the sports equipment for the final rehab. I've been round the place. They've got archery, basketball and shooting equipment.'

A dizzy-looking young nurse who didn't look as though she'd make it through her first year piped, 'Oh, shooting! One of the staff nurses in theatre does that as a hobby.' She then looked pointedly at Antonia.

'Let's concentrate on immediate post-traumatic nursing procedures, shall we?' Antonia ended the meeting and headed towards the sunroom. She knew Eddy wouldn't be awkward about moving. Rolf, on the other hand, wouldn't be pleased. But then, she had no choice. This was typical of a nurse's day—management by crisis.

CHAPTER NINE

'THE ward needs your co-operation, Eddy,' Antonia began gently. She gave a brief account of the new patient and why he had to be accommodated on the orthopaedic ward.

'That's fine by me, Staff.' Eddy didn't look put out. He was lying prone on his bed stretching his hip flexors. Then he rolled over. 'What sort of ward will I be going to?'

'A surgical one. It's mixed——' She had hardly said the word.

'Whoopee! You mean I might be lying next to a beautiful young girl?'

'No way.' Antonia couldn't help laughing. 'You'll be in a four-bedder small section with men. But yes, there will be women. But not so close that it'll affect your blood-pressure.'

'Spoilsports!' Eddy grinned widely.

Michael spoke up. 'I don't think Eddy should go. He looked very frail this morning. Send me— I'm willing.'

'You're incorrigible!' Antonia tapped the end of Michael's bed. 'You're staying right here.'

There was a flurry of activity to pack Eddy's

belongings and prepare the bed for the new admission.

As Eddy was being wheeled away by a porter she felt a pang. Had she done absolutely everything to ensure his safe transfer to the surgical ward? She thought she had. But niggling in the back of her mind was the old guilt. She still believed that by arguing with Rolf on the morning of Eddy's accident, she had wasted time, and that somehow it was partly her fault that he had ended up an above- rather than a through-knee amputee.

Timid fingers tugged at her white apron. Michael's normally relaxed features were taut. 'This new bloke. . .is he likely to die?'

'No,' she reassured him quickly. Like all nurses she knew that patients feared the fact that they might have to be near the dying. 'No, he's already got a bed booked in another hospital.' She laid her hand across his forearm. 'You've been a marvellous help with Eddy. Everyone's noticed how you've helped to keep his spirits up.'

'That's not hard. There's something likeable about him, even though he can be a bit dozy at times. I hope he comes back soon.'

Antonia was utterly exhausted when she got home that evening. She lay down on the chester-field, only to rest for a few minutes, but two hours later she was awoken from a deep sleep by the ringing of her doorbell.

Making her way downstairs, she felt faintly sick, as if she'd been woken suddenly in the middle of the night. She opened the door to Lindain.

He stood there all smiles with a bunch of white carnations in one hand and a box of chocolates in the other.

'Did I wake you, darling? I'm sorry.'

'Oh, hello,' she said sleepily.

In her sitting-room she faced him on the chesterfield, still fighting off the effects of sleep.

'I've been very unfair to you, Antonia darling. I've neglected you dreadfully. Of course, the upcoming exams haven't helped.'

She rubbed her eyes. He was trying very hard to apologise, she knew.

'And you're right, you're not properly engaged until you've got a ring.' He produced a red leather box that was slightly worn at the edges. 'It's a beautiful solitaire diamond, and an antique at least.'

She stared at it. A few months ago she would have been over the moon to receive a ring like this. But somehow things had changed between them.

'Well, say something, darling!' Lindain sounded a little jaded. 'These antique rings are terribly expensive. But I was clever—I got it from a pawnshop, it's amazing what bargains you can pick up there.'

Not everything Lindain said permeated through Antonia's mind. 'I'll have to think about it. . .' She looked up into his shocked eyes. 'Just give me a bit of time.'

He kissed her, but as his lips came down on hers she felt unmoved. She had known passionate kisses—but they had come from Rolf.

Lindain leaned back and suppressed a sigh. 'You're right to be really sure before we get married. But don't keep me waiting too long, Antonia. When we're man and wife we'll travel the world. America's the place—that's where medics really make the money.'

Lindain produced a gold chain. 'While you're making up your mind, wear the ring around your neck.'

The chain was beautiful, like the ring. Lindain was making such an effort, it seemed as if she was being unfair. Suddenly she remembered all his kindness after her parents' death.

'It's the right time to get hitched,' he went on. 'McMaster's about to do it. He had some gorgeous brunette with him today and he'd had the engagement ring made smaller to fit her finger. He gave her an antique ring too.'

Something like a stab went through Antonia's heart.

'He's engaged, then? That's definite?'

'They looked the perfect picture of the happy couple together.'

It hit her then. She acknowledged that she had wanted Rolf, and passionately. But he'd never been free.

'We won't be short of a bob or two,' Lindain continued. 'Especially when your inheritance comes through, when you're twenty-five.'

'Thirty-five,' she corrected him. But as she did so she was thinking of Rolf, so she didn't see the shocked expression that Lindain carefully hid.

'I'll wear the ring as you say, Lindain. And I'll think about it. I don't imagine I'll take long to make up my mind.' He helped her secure the chain about her neck, and she suddenly felt the weight of the heavy old gold.

The following morning Antonia was again in charge of the ward. Shortly after nine-thirty a thunderous-looking Rolf strode up to her. He was still in his theatre greens and his mask was slung beneath his chin.

'Where's Sister Cook?' he demanded.

'It's her day off. May I help you?' She suspected that he'd just found out about Eddy's transfer.

'Were you in charge of this ward early this morning, then?'

'Yes, I was.' She spoke slowly. He wasn't going to browbeat her. The transfer had been her only course of action.

'Then I'll speak to you in private.'

In her own time Antonia organised her junior staff nurse to take over the drug round. Then she led Rolf to the kitchen. Sister's sitting-room would have been more suitable, but there was a patient in it.

The door was slammed shut. 'My God, you're a cool customer!' he bit out. 'I imagine you don't know where Eddy is right now?'

'I don't know exactly——'

'You're damn right, because he's in recovery in theatre!'

She felt herself go cold. 'Whatever for?'

Rolf's eyes were metallic. 'Because you obviously can't keep track of the patients under your care. It seems he took it into his head to go walkabout, and he fell from the top of some stairs into the main corridor.'

She covered her mouth with her hand.

'Yes, you may well look upset now. He smashed his stump and ripped his wound open again. I've just finished sewing him up.'

'Oh, no!'

'Where was your mind, Toni, when you were running the ward this morning?'

'He wasn't here. I transferred him yesterday.'

'You what?' Rolf's voice was barely controlled. 'Haven't I dinned it into your head enough? It's vital for psychological rehabilitation to keep the medical personnel constant.'

'It wasn't my fault,' she hit back. 'I had no choice. We had an emergency admission——'

'Surely there was some space on the ward? You could have kept my patient here.'

He was being thoroughly unreasonable. She felt her temper mounting. 'And where do you suggest I should have put him? Hanging from a hammock, suspended from the ceiling?'

'Don't be so damned insolent!'

There was an uneasy silence.

'What a damn mess!' Rolf thrust his hand to his forehead and shook his head slowly. 'And by the grace of God, some good came out of all this confusion.'

She didn't understand. She was about to ask what good could possibly have happened, but his face took on a determined look.

'Which ward?' he demanded.

'Four.'

'A bloody surgical ward, of course!' He jerked open the door and set off.

Almost immediately a third-year nurse

entered the kitchen. 'I've just had a phone call from theatre. Sister there was about to warn you that McMaster was in a foul mood. People tried to tell him that Eddy was outside ward four when he fell, but he wouldn't let anyone speak when he was operating. He called for absolute silence.'

'I've sorted that out,' Antonia said weakly. 'I think he's on his way to bawl out ward four right now.'

The third-year explained, 'Eddy says it's all his fault. He wanted to practise stairs. But of course McMaster didn't hear this, because Eddy was under the anaesthetic by the time he was changed and ready to operate.' The nurse burst into tears. 'It had to be our Eddy, didn't it?'

Antonia put her arm about her. She felt like crying too, but someone had to remain calm, she still had to run the ward.

Later she looked up suddenly from her paper-work and saw Rolf striding towards her. Oh, no, here he comes again! she thought.

'Another word in private, please,' he said brusquely.

This time she followed him to the kitchen.

'I'm sorry, Toni, I shouldn't have bawled you out like that. Sister on Four explained. And it seems it was nobody's fault. Eddy crept out to the stairwell during the change-over report. The door to Sister's office was closed, so no one saw him go. It wasn't your fault.'

Then very considerately he said, 'You look white, Toni. Perhaps you'd better sit down.'

All the steel reserve that had kept her in control melted away. 'But it is my fault!' She buried her face in her hands. 'It's all my fault that he's an above- rather than a through-knee amp——' She began to sob.

'What stupid idea is this that's got stuck in your head?' His voice was soft and close to her face.

'It's true—I know. The morning I drove you here to operate on him, I argued with you. I wasted time. That's why the site of amputation had to be revised——'

'No, that's not what happened.' She felt his arms about her. 'Eddy was given a through-knee surgical procedure only to cut him free from his cab. The casualty officer did the operation that way because it was the quickest, and because it didn't involve cutting through muscle.'

His voice was so soothing, his words were so welcome. He was absolving her from blame. She pressed her head against his chest.

'Eddy had a crush fracture through his knee joint, the end of his femur was shattered. He would never have been able to use a through-knee prosthesis.'

He tipped her tear-stained face up to his. But somehow she couldn't look into his eyes.

'You've felt guilty all along—that's why you've been so over-protective to him.'

She couldn't answer.

He sighed deeply. 'I suppose I made you feel guilty. I scolded you viciously when I first recognised you. It never occurred to me that you'd taken such blame upon yourself. I'm truly sorry.'

When he held her tighter she wished he would hold her like that forever.

'But it's not all bad news.' His voice was soft against her ear. 'Between the ripped muscle and some fascia I found a foreign body. It must have lodged there at the time of the accident. Some inflammation surrounded it.'

Antonia listened intently.

'If Eddy hadn't opened his wound again it might have been months before the source of infection revealed itself, and during that time a lot of damage could have been done. So you see, Eddy's fall was a piece of luck.'

Antonia felt the weight of guilt drop from her like a stone. She looked into Rolf's eyes.

Rolf continued 'And it was lucky for Eddy too when I commandeered you. The casualty officer would have performed the revised amputation in theatre. But I've had far more experience, so Eddy got the better deal.' He spoke slowly to make his point. 'You were Eddy's good luck, Toni. That's what you must remember now.'

'I'm so glad. . .' She felt tears welling up again, and Rolf's finger brushed them away.

'And chance has placed another ace card. . . It's brought you and me together. Can't you see, Toni, I'm the one who's always on the spot when you're in distress? You ran into me when you were frightened in Physio, I was with you the night you had the panic attack after the Summer Ball. The fates are pushing us together. We're meant for each other—don't fight it.'

Tension spread throughout her body as the talk became personal.

'Let me come to your flat tonight, Toni. I'll help you pack your things and you can come and live with me at Hawksworth.'

He sounded so sincere. And she wouldn't have hesitated if she hadn't known about Kay and his engagement. How could he be so fickle?

Slowly she turned away from him and walked to the kitchen sink. She splashed cold water on her face, then found he was holding a paper kitchen towel for her. If he wasn't so nice like this, it wouldn't hurt so much.

'Thanks for explaining everything. . . I'd better get back to the ward.'

He caught her arm. 'Come to me any time—you know where I live.'

It was so hard to walk away. But she did it without looking back.

CHAPTER TEN

AT THE end of her shift Antonia visited Eddy on ward four. But he was dozing peacefully, so she left him.

'Tell him I popped up to see him,' she told Sister Williams.

'Your consultant's got the most fiery temper I've ever known!' Sister shook her head as they walked to her office. 'I don't envy you having to work for McMaster.'

'Oh, but he's only like that because he cares passionately about his patients,' Antonia defended.

Sister smiled, then promised to give Eddy Antonia's message.

All day intense heat had beaten down on the town, and when Antonia got home to her flat it was unbearably hot. It was as if the weight of the sky was literally pressing hard down everywhere.

Confusion reigned uppermost in her mind. Lindain had proposed and Rolf had asked her to be his mistress. She wanted Rolf, but she refused to be used. She tried Lindain's ring on for size.

It was difficult to push on to her finger, but she managed it, and there she let it stay, even though she felt unsure.

On impulse she decided to go into town and buy some cotton tops. But, by chance, she caught the bus going to the city some ten miles away. Not wanting to wait for another bus, she decided to shop in the city.

The leading department store was wonderfully cooled by the air-conditioning, so she stayed longer than she had intended and ate supper in the restaurant.

When she finally walked to the bus-stop it was nearly nine, and the sky was ominously overcast.

The rain came suddenly, drenching the queue. Everyone huddled up under the shelter, but a few, including Antonia, were left outside. They heard far-off thunder and someone said, 'They've had one hell of a storm along the main road. I suppose it's moving this way now.'

Antonia shuddered, then she heard a familiar voice. 'I thought it was you in my headlights. Come on, I've got the Range Rover, I'm taking you home.'

Before she had time to think Rolf had bundled her into the vehicle, and they were back in the main stream of city traffic.

'You wouldn't have got very far on that bus, Toni,' he told her. 'Local radio have issued a traffic flash—a tree's down. It's completely blocked the main road.'

In spite of her reservations she was glad to be riding with Rolf.

'We'll head for home via Stoneton village.' He turned off the main road and they drove through the winding narrow streets.

'This is a six-mile detour, isn't it?' she queried.

'Yes. But it'll be quicker this way.'

They drove further out into the open country-side; it was completely black outside. No city street lights here.

Without warning a rainstorm hit the vehicle and they were buffeted about on the back lanes. Rolf pulled to a halt as the storm advanced. The sky was green-black, thick clouds whirled over-head. Booming thunder echoed outside and fork lightning rent the air, lighting up the isolated landscape.

Antonia felt his arm steal around her shoulders. 'Are you afraid?'

She answered truthfully, 'No, I enjoy watch-ing.' What she meant was, she wasn't afraid with him.

At the climax of the storm there was an almighty crack and a huge fork of lightning appeared to their right.

'By God, that was close!' muttered Rolf.

'Did you see if it struck anything?' Antonia peered through the car windows.

'No. Somewhere behind that hill, though. The road curves around that way, so we'll see when we get going.'

During the next few minutes the sky ceased its whirling and the thunder became more distant and rolled away. The night was still pitch-black, though.

Putting the car in gear, Rolf said, 'Watch the road up ahead, Toni. That last lightning crack might have brought a tree down.'

The pelting rain had now subsided to a soft patter. Squeaking and creaking, the windscreen wipers worked over the windscreen, so it was hard to be sure when she saw a black shape moving on the road ahead.

'Stop!' Antonia was right to have called out. A man's face, contorted with pain, came into view. He was crawling in the road and he had raised his left arm to halt them.

Rolf and Antonia jumped out immediately, and only then Antonia saw the cottage by the roadside. It was a solitary house in this bleak landscape and the lightning had struck it. A large tree had crashed through the roof and into the building.

'I'm a doctor—where are you hurt?' Rolf squatted by the man.

'Leave me, leave me,' he rasped. 'I'm all right.' He was panting. 'It's my little girl. . .she's in the bedroom upstairs.'

Antonia saw that the man could not move his legs, and she noticed the tracks he had made in the mud on the ground. He must have literally crawled on his belly to the road.

Before she knew what was happening Rolf had brought his medical bag and a heavy-duty torch from the car. 'We'll find your daughter, don't worry. What's her name?'

'Sophy.'

Rolf dragged Antonia along. Part of the front of the cottage was down, so they had to pick their way over the rubble. She was glad she had Rolf to hang on to.

In the beam of the torch they saw the tree, unnaturally lying in the interior of the cottage. It almost completely blocked the staircase, which was panelled off and completely enclosed.

The door to the stairs was slightly open; Rolf tested the tree for steadiness, then climbed on the trunk. 'It's no good, I can't get through this narrow opening.' He pulled the door hard, but it wouldn't budge against the tree.

He turned to Antonia. 'You're slight enough, you could squeeze through.' She felt his hands guide her to the narrow opening. She looked inside. It was deadly black. Panic got a hold of

her and she began to shudder. 'I can't. . . I can't
go in there!'

As if he understood without further questioning Rolf picked his way outside and called to the
man, 'Have you got a ladder somewhere here?
We might be able to reach the bedrooms that
way.'

'My brother borrowed them today. . .
Goddammit!'

The little girl must have heard her father's
voice, for she began to scream.

'We're coming, darling!' the man shouted back.

Then Rolf was holding Antonia's shoulders,
'You've got to go up there, Toni. You've got to
bring the child down.' Again he turned her to
the partly open door.

Again she turned away in terror as her heart
raced and her legs trembled.

From somewhere he produced a ball of string.
'Look, Toni, I'm going to tie this string around
your waist. It'll act like an umbilical cord.
Remember, the early astronauts used one when
they left the space craft?'

She felt him secure the string. 'No, I can't.
I can't do it! You don't know what you're
asking——' She couldn't enter that pitch-black
tunnel. She would suffocate—she would surely
die.

'You must try, Toni——'

'No, I can't.' She shook her head.

Something was being pressed into her hand. 'Take this—it's my lucky coin. I have it with me when I operate. Here, I've put it in your breast pocket, it'll safeguard you, and you'll be able to do it.'

He was guiding her to the door again. The child had stopped screaming, and a pathetic whimpering was all that could be heard.

Rolf's voice was firm as he lifted her hands to the muscles of her neck. 'Feel these muscles,' he ordered. 'Feel how strong you are. You're strong, Toni. Get the child.'

The torch was in her hand, he had manoeuvred her into the opening at the bottom of the staircase. She froze. The beam of light was like the beams in the coalminers' helmets.

Rolf's voice was behind her. She knew she must go up and find the child. Inwardly she struggled for control, but the old panc images were strong.

'Go a quarter of the way up the stairs, Toni.'

That voice somehow gave her the strength to move her legs. They felt leaden. The child was still whimpering, and the sound seemed to come from a long way off. She must try and remember she was not down the mine. It was difficult, because over everything there hovered a feeling of unreality.

'Go halfway up the stairs, Toni. My voice will go with you.'

She made it halfway, then three quarters. Then at the top of the stairs she stood frozen.

'Find the child, Toni. Call her name.'

At first her throat felt so tight she could not speak. Then, 'Sophy, I've come to take you to Daddy.'

Magic words. The child ran out of the darkness and gripped Toni's legs. She was trembling and sobbing, 'Where's Daddy?'

The old pictures of the young miner dying faded from Antonia's mind. Here was a living child, and they were in a cottage.

'Bring the child to me, Toni.' Rolf's voice was a firm command.

It was easier going downstairs than it had been going up. And suddenly she saw Rolf's face. He lifted Sophy and told her that her father was outside, then the father called and she ran to him. There was nothing physically wrong with her, she had only been shocked.

Then strong arms pulled Antonia from the darkness, and she was held fast against Rolf's chest. 'That's my brave girl,' he said. 'And only I know how much it cost you to do that.' He kissed her face passionately.

Reluctantly he held her away and untied the string that had bound them. The torch was between them, and its light shone up, illuminating his face. He was a study in deep shadow and golden light. And to Antonia he was the most wonderful, most handsome man in the world.

'We have patients outside, but our time will come later.' He led her out of the cottage.

Swiftly he examined the man. 'Fractured tib and fib of both legs. Luckily there's no bone displacement and the fractures aren't comminuted.' Addressing the man directly, 'You've broken both shins, but not badly. I've got some air splints, and a stretcher. My nurse and I will fix you up in splints, then we'll head for the Royal.'

'A doctor, a nurse, and a Range Rover ambulance. . .and all in the middle of nowhere just when we needed them, Sophy!' The man ruffled his daughter's hair. 'Don't say you don't believe in guardian angels any more, little girl.'

Rolf added, 'I think a few guardian angels have been working overtime tonight.' When he smiled into Antonia's eyes, she felt a glow of warmth because she knew that special smile was just for her.

They lifted the man into the back of the Range Rover, and Sophy nestled against his chest.

In the front seat Rolf deliberately dropped his ignition keys. Antonia picked them up and handed them over with her left hand.

As he held her hand tightly, Rolf's fingers caught against Lindain's engagement ring.

His expression changed instantly to a look of deep hurt. He turned abruptly away, and with a stiff reserve said, 'We'll be at the Royal in about twenty minutes.'

She couldn't bear that look of pain that made his mouth so ugly. She wanted to tear the ring off, throw it out of the window and tell him that now she knew she could never love anyone but him.

The ring refused to come off. It stuck fast. She couldn't tell Rolf because the man and his child were only feet away—it was not the time for explanations.

At the Royal she raced ahead and organised some porters from Casualty who ran down to Rolf with a trolley. The man was speedily checked by the casualty officer and then sent to X-Ray.

Before she could talk to Rolf, the charge nurse waylaid him and appeared to speak gravely.

Rolf caught Antonia's eye, then said something to the charge nurse and dashed away.

'Sit down, I've some bad news.' The charge nurse laid his large hand on her shoulder.

'Someone in my family must be hurt?' She knew that look.

'You're engaged to Dr Smythe, aren't you?'

'Yes.'

'It sounds very serious, but I don't think it's that bad. He's got a bullet wound in his leg.'

Antonia was incredulous. 'A *bullet*? How was he shot?'

'He was carrying bullets for his pistol-shooting in the boot of his car. Another car rammed the back, the petrol tank caught fire and exploded, and the bullets literally flew everywhere.'

'Are you sure it's Dr Lindain Smythe? Pistol-shooting isn't his hobby.'

The charge nurse's face went blank. 'I'm sorry, it's him all right.'

'Where did the bullet enter?'

Again there was a pause. 'In the femoral triangle. But don't worry, McMaster's going to operate, and, as you know, he's had experience with gunshot wounds in Northern Ireland.'

'Was there a distal pulse?'

Antonia had to know. If no blood was being pumped to the leg by the main femoral artery then the chance of gangrene was great. And amputation might be a possibility.

'No femoral pulse,' came the unwelcome reply. Then, 'Let me get you a cup of tea.'

Antonia took a few sips, then said, 'I'd rather wait alone. I'll be in the staff nurses' sitting-room when there's any news. Thank you.'

She was grateful that there was no one else in

the sitting-room, for her mind was in turmoil. The ring on her finger was still tight. How could she leave Lindain now, especially after his help after her bereavement? No, she had to stand by him. And what was the use of loving Rolf? None. He belonged to Kay.

It seemed forever before she heard a gentle tapping on the door, and Rolf appeared in his theatre greens. She ran to him.

'How is he?' she asked anxiously.

'I found the bullet next to the femoral artery. It hadn't injured the vessel, and when I removed it the segmentary spasm stopped and the artery, which had contracted to the size of a small knitting needle, dilated to its normal size.' He spoke as an automaton.

'Then he's all right?'

Rolf's face was grim. 'Perfectly.'

'Where is he?'

'On the private ward.'

'I must see him!' Antonia brushed past Rolf. All she could think of was Lindain and his lucky escape. She heard Rolf calling, but she wouldn't listen.

Night Sister on the private ward stifled a yawn as Antonia entered the ward.

Antonia said, 'May I see Dr Smythe? Which room is he in?'

'Oh, he's a very popular young doctor!' Sister's smile was broad. 'He's fine——'

'But which room?' Antonia knew she was being abrupt, but she wanted to see Lindain.

'Number two.'

'May I go in for a short time, please? I won't stay for long. I'm his fiancée.' She turned to go, she couldn't wait for Sister's answer.

'No. . .not now!' Sister sounded confused.

Through the porthole window of room two Antonia saw Lindain and another woman. The woman was bending low over him, kissing him deeply with what was obviously a lover's kiss.

Sister's voice was close behind. 'I'm sorry you had to find out like this, dear. But if I had a gorgeous consultant eating his heart out for me, I wouldn't fret one bit.'

Antonia turned abruptly and saw that Sister obviously knew all about Lindain.

'That's Staff Nurse from theatre,' the older woman explained. 'But there've been many——'

Antonia couldn't bear to hear any more. It was unbearable to have been so completely deceived and for everyone but herself to know. What a fool she'd been!

Back in the sitting-room she soaped her ring finger at the washbasin and tore off the engagement ring. Now many scenes from the past came back clearly to her. She remembered Lindain's proposal and the fact that the ring had come from a pawnshop. Then she was furious.

In her handbag she found an old envelope and a piece of paper. On the paper she hastily scratched the sign of the pawnbroker—the three hanging balls—and by it she put an exclamation mark. The message was very vulgar but very satisfying!

She thrust the ring and the drawing into the envelope and marched to the pigeonholes outside the doctors' sitting-room. That posted, she now had to think about going home. She felt absolutely drained.

But as she drew the strap of her shoulder-bag across her body it caused something hard to press into her left breast. It was the lucky coin that Rolf had given her to help her rescue Sophy.

She took it out and stared at it. He had said that it brought him luck, and that he never operated without it. In all fairness she should return it quickly.

She was lucky to find a taxi outside the hospital and soon she was at Hawksworth.

The heavy door was ajar, so she walked straight in. The hall was lit. She heard a man whistling. The sound was haunting and infinitely sad. It was a short refrain repeated over and over again. Following the sound, she came to the drawing-room.

It was in darkness, and Rolf's silhouette was clearly visible against the squared pattern of the french windows.

He did not see her. He stood looking out at the night sky, which was partly clouded, partly studded with stars. His shoulders drooped.

Somehow his whistling pained her. She called his name softly.

Swiftly he was by her side and the lights were full on. 'What's the problem, Toni? Is Smythe OK?'

'Perfectly.' She sounded more jaded than she had meant. 'He's with Staff Nurse from theatre.'

Rolf looked closely into her face. 'It'll hurt for a while, then it'll fade. I know.'

She didn't want his sympathy. 'I've come to return your lucky coin.' She held it out for him.

He took it, studied it for a moment, then flipped it in the air and let it fall to the floor. It rolled for a few yards, then fell flat.

'It has no value, except its face value.'

'But I thought you never operated without it?'

'I only told you that to get you through an impossible situation, Toni.' There was an awkward silence. Then he said, 'You look exhausted. I'll take you home.'

The events of the day spun in her head. She

let him guide her to the front door. She hardly noticed anything, certainly not the fact that he switched off the drawing-room light.

At the front door he turned abruptly and barred her exit. 'I'm not taking you home, Toni. . .because this is your home. I want you to marry me and live here.'

She looked up incredulously. 'But you're engaged to Kay—I know. You bought her an antique engagement ring.'

'Wherever did you get that nonsense from?'

She didn't answer; she was trying hard to think.

'Toni, sweetheart, I've told you before, Kay and I are old friends. . . We both share a bitter past.' He took a deep breath. 'You see, it was my wife who ran off and married her husband.'

She wanted to believe him. 'But what about the engagement ring?'

'The ring that her fiancé gave her was antique. The stone was loose in its setting, and I took it to a jeweller for her, that's all.'

Had Lindain lied about that too? Antonia considered the idea for a while, then she knew she didn't care any longer.

'I'm free, Toni, so are you,' Rolf went on. 'You're free to marry anyone.'

She looked steadily at him. 'No, I'm not free. . .' His face darkened. 'Because I feel bound to you. Ever since you made me face the dark and conquer my fear.'

He covered her face in kisses. 'That was the most difficult thing I could ever make you do. But I had no choice. Confronting a fear like that could have been psychologically very dangerous, I would have preferred you to have had treatment under controlled conditions and by gradual desensitisation.'

'No, I'm glad you made me do it. I feel I'm cured, and that I could do anything now.' She nestled against his chest.

'Do you trust me, Toni? Are you willing to try and see?'

'Yes,' she replied simply.

He switched off the hall light and the place was plunged into darkness. She heard him moving away and leaving her alone, but she felt no fear. She was in control.

'How do you feel now?' His voice came softly across the void.

'Fine. . . I'm not trembling.'

She thought she heard him move again, but she couldn't be sure. His voice floated down to her as from a great height.

'And now. . .?'

'I feel just the same. . . OK.'

'Come to me!' he called.

She blinked, trying to adjust her eyes. Feeling

her way with her hands outstretched, she found the banister at the bottom of the staircase. Then, still holding on, she walked up quickly. She stumbled once, but she didn't fall.

At the top of the stairs she reached out for him. But the night was empty.

'Where are you now?' It was tantalising to have him concealed by the dark.

'Outside our bedroom.'

Groping her way across the landing, she walked towards his voice. Then suddenly she was in his arms and being hugged tightly. 'A complete cure, thank God,' he murmured. 'Is your heart racing?'

'Yes, but that's because I'm with you.'

He chuckled, then spoke seriously. 'I'm glad. A heart that beats in fear is forever caged.'

'I'm free, because I consulted the right doctor,' she sighed.

She felt him laugh against her body.

Then she explained the past to him. 'Lindain's heart was full of lies. But now I know your heart is full of love. I don't know that I ever really loved Lindain, certainly not the way I love you. But he was so nice after my parents' death. And at that time Rupert had left home and I suddenly felt terribly alone. . .and I was becoming aware that my fear of the dark was getting worse. I suppose I felt I owed him a debt of gratitude.'

Rolf stroked the fringe off her forehead.

'I fell in love with your beauty, Toni, when you first came to my outpatients clinic. And I fell in love with your obvious caring when you warned me that Mrs Cluny was about to do battle on behalf of Nigel.'

She felt his breath fanning her face and she traced the line of his upper lip with her index finger. He took her fingertips and kissed them.

'I'm a jealous man, Toni—I know it's a fault of mine. But when I fall in love it's a very intense thing. It was too intense for my first wife. . . It was that intense emotion that made me bawl you out when I saw you straightening Smythe's collar. I couldn't bear to think of you with a heartless man like that.'

Her eyes met his. 'I'll never give you any cause to be jealous. And if your love is intense forever, then I'll consider myself supremely blessed.'

He bent his head and kissed her passionately.

In the bedroom he flicked on the light and led her to the bed. 'Do you remember this?' he asked.

On the head of the brass bedstead there was a red ribbon. 'It's the one I gave you tied to the wooden spoon.' Antonia giggled.

'Right.' He fingered it. 'It means I've really won first prize, because you're here with me now.'

'You're crazy! But I knew that from the first time I met you.' She remembered that old scene and smiled. 'I thought you were wearing a T-shirt that said "Bare Barber-Surgeon".'

'Aha! You mean "Paré Barber-Surgeon".'

'Yes, but the T-shirt was filthy at the time, and the letters were obscured.'

He turned her round to face him. 'Kay will be pleased! She gave me that T-shirt one Christmas just for fun.' His eyes twinkled, then he grinned wickedly. 'Bare barber surgeon. . . I like the idea, and it can so easily be arranged.'

He pulled off his clothes, then undressed her reverently. Throughout the night they explored each other's bodies and found ecstasy. And Antonia knew that she would never be afraid again. Because even in the darkest night, all she had to do was think of Rolf and it was as if all the lights in her head blazed on at once.

Mills & Boon

Discover the thrill of 4 Exciting
Medical Romances – FREE

FREE
BOOKS FOR YOU

In the exciting world of modern
medicine, the emotions of true love
have an added drama. Now you can
experience four of these
unforgettable romantic tales of passion
and heartbreak FREE – and look forward to
a regular supply of Mills & Boon
Medical Romances delivered direct to your door!

🍃 🍃 🍃

Turn the page for details of 2 extra
free gifts, and how to apply.

An Irresistible Offer from Mills & Boon

Here's an offer from Mills & Boon to become a regular reader of Medical Romances. To welcome you, we'd like you to have four books, a cuddly teddy and a special MYSTERY GIFT, all absolutely free and without obligation.

Then, every two months you could look forward to receiving 6 more **brand new** Medical Romances for £1.35 each, delivered direct to your door, post and packing free. Plus our newsletter featuring author news, competitions, special offers, and lots more.

This invitation comes with no strings attached. You can cancel or suspend your subscription at any time, and still keep your free books and gifts.

Its so easy. Send no money now. Simply fill in the coupon below and post it at once to -

**Mills & Boon Reader Service, FREEPOST,
PO Box 236, Croydon, Surrey CR9 9EL**

NO STAMP REQUIRED

- -

YES! Please rush me my 4 Free Medical Romances and 2 Free Gifts! Please also reserve me a Reader Service Subscription. If I decide to subscribe, I can look forward to receiving 6 brand new Medical Romances every two months for just £8.10, delivered direct to my door. Post and packing is free, and there's a free Mills & Boon Newsletter. If I choose not to subscribe I shall write to you within 10 days - I can keep the books and gifts whatever I decide. I can cancel or suspend my subscription at any time. I am over 18.

EP90D

Name (Mr/Mrs/Ms) _____

Address _____

_____

_____ Postcode _____

Signature _____

mps
MAILING
PREFERENCE
SERVICE

4 MEDICAL ROMANCES
AND 2 FREE GIFTS
From Mills & Boon

Capture all the excitement, intrigue and emotion of the busy medical world by accepting four FREE Medical Romances, plus a FREE cuddly teddy and special mystery gift. Then if you choose, go on to enjoy 6 more exciting Medical Romances every two months! Send the coupon below at once to:

**MILLS & BOON READER SERVICE, FREEPOST
PO BOX 236, CROYDON, SURREY CR9 9EL.**
No stamp required

✂ - ✂

YES! Please rush me my 4 Free Medical Romances and 2 Free Gifts! Please also reserve me a Reader Service Subscription. If I decide to subscribe, I can look forward to receiving 6 Medical Romances every two months for just £8.10 delivered direct to my door. Post and packing is free, and there's a free Mills & Boon Newsletter. If I choose not to subscribe I shall write to you within 10 days – I can keep the books and gifts whatever I decide. I can cancel or suspend my subscription at any time. I am over 18.

EP89D

Name (Mr/Mrs/Ms) _____

Address _____

_____

_____ Postcode _____

Signature _____